CARLOS

CARLOS

Porn Star Brothers Book 1

L.J. DIVA

★ Royal Star Publishing ★

Chances is an imprint of Royal Star Publishing
www.royalstarpublishing.com.au

This Collector's Edition paperback published in 2018
All Rights Reserved, Copyright ©L.J. Diva 2018

Trade Paperback ISBN: 978-1-925683-40-0
Case Laminate Hardcover ISBN: 978-1-922307-27-9
E-Book ISBN: 978-1-925683-39-4
A catalogue record for this book is available from the National
Library of Australia.

Cover design: Royal Star Publishing and Odyssey Books
Cover photos: CURAphotography/Shutterstock.com
Typesetting in Minion Pro by Royal Star Publishing

 Dedications

In 2014 a vague idea to write a book about a porn star came to me. In 2015 the idea brewed and grew and when my idol, Jackie Collins, passed away, the idea flourished with a vengeance. Jackie Collins is the only inspiration in my life when it comes to writing. She had the passion, the brains, the ballsy rollicking attitude, and the kind of life that made me want to *be* her. Without her, these books would not exist, for I would not have had the inspiration to follow in the same 'write whatever you want' league. Without her, I will continue trying to write the kind of books she wrote. Real, ballsy, and bonkbustingly good.

Jackie, the Porn Star Brothers book series is dedicated to you as so many of my other books are. I thank you for the inspiration you have given me and hope you continue giving me, to go on and write more. I hope that you are well and having a good laugh wherever you are. I miss you and will continue doing so. Sometimes I think I feel you egging me on with my writing. Maybe that's true, and maybe it's just my rampant imagination; the same imagination that has given me the books I have written so far in my life. And sometimes, I really wished I could be you. You will forever be my idol and inspiration and I thank you. RIP, Miss Jackie C.

And to the three Stefanovic brothers, Carlos, Pedro, and Tomas, without whom I would not have had names for my porn stars.

CARLOS

June 1977

"Ohhh, Carlos, you're such a stud…ugh…ugh…ugh." The blonde Australian girl groaned as she lay underneath the five-foot-ten frame of the man fucking her. She was losing her mind. No man had ever made her orgasm this way before. In fact, no man had ever made her orgasm; period.

Carlos Stephanopoulos made one final thrust into the young girl beneath him and casually rolled off, running his hand through his silken shoulder length golden-brown hair that was as thick as any stud's hair should be. Sweat trickled from his brow as he leant back against the pile of pillows behind him, and he grabbed a bottle of beer from the bedside table and took a swig.

"Oh, Carlos." The blonde snuggled up to him, stroking his manly golden chest. "That was *so* good." She pulled his arm around her but he pulled it back.

After flinging the sheet back from the bed, he grabbed his shorts from the floor and pulled them on.

"Glad you think so." His accent was a healthy mix of Greek and Australian, having been born and raised in the land down under.

His father, Spiros, had immigrated to Australia in 1950 where he met Jenny, the young Australian girl he would later propose to and marry. They had Carlos nine months after the wedding with his brothers soon following, and they led a very Australian life in a small town inland from the coast of New South Wales.

When Carlos was fourteen, his father packed them up and moved them all to Greece because *his* father had died, leaving Spiros Stephanopoulos the family business.

At first, Carlos and his brothers hated being wrenched away from the only home they'd known, but while the hankering for Australia stayed with them, they had grown to love Greece, especially the islands of Mykonos and Santorini where they spent their summers, with Carlos getting it on with every bit of skirt he could get his hands on. Oh, yes, their Greek island home was certainly providing a bountiful plethora of young, tanned and incredibly gullible beauties.

Carlos slid on his tank top with the resort's logo on the left breast. He worked at the biggest resort on Mykonos as a summer fill-in and fill in he did. He filled all the girls he could and enjoyed himself immensely. No commitment, no worries. Just summers filled with hot blaring sun and hot horny women.

Of course, *sometimes* he dipped into the pool of older female tourists and, of course, they *insisted* on paying him for his time and energy. The first time that had happened he'd been shocked that a woman was offering him money for services rendered. But after hearing the other workers at the resort say the older ladies liked to pay for extra services, he had dipped his cock more frequently, and now older women were a regular thing and it paid well. The young ones…well, they were just a bit of fluff on the side.

Ah, the Greek islands…so full of beautiful, wealthy women. It was a great place to live!

"Carlos," purred the girl who was young, lithe and full of bounce. "Let's do that again." She knelt on the bed behind him and wrapped her arms around his waist, sliding her hand into his shorts.

He grabbed her hand, removed it, and gave it back to her. "That's enough. I need to get back to work." He stepped into his sandals and headed for the door to the holiday apartment she shared with her friends.

They were on holiday from Australia and Carlos had liked chatting with them to get word from back home, hearing how things had changed since he'd been there. But sometimes, younger girls could be clingy, and this one was being clingy right now.

"Carlos…"

He stopped and turned in the doorway.

She stood naked at the end of the bed. "Don't you want more of this?" Her left forefinger was on her lips while her right hand slid into the bushy thatch between her legs.

The sight of her doing that turned him off. "Nah, I'm done."

Why do so many girls try so hard? he thought as he strode down the cobbled walkways of Mykonos. *They come off so desperately needy, yet the older women always have so much more confidence.* Not necessarily as much stamina, but far more confidence than he'd ever seen in any of the young girls he bedded.

He made it back to the resort just as his lunch break was over and took his position at the spray booth. He always had long lines of beautiful women waiting to be sprayed down with coconut oil before baking to a crisp in the sun. At two dollars a pop, he kept half of what he earned, and it was a thriving business all on its own. Like now, there had been no one waiting at the tent when he'd walked up, but now people, mainly gorgeous women and a few gay men he recognised, were swarming into a line that weaved down the beach waiting for his magic hands to do their work.

"Who's up for a spray?" he called out and received cheers in return. "Well, hello lovely lady, step right over here and turn around slowly." He led his first customer to the left of the tent where everyone stood on a round mat on the sand. He sprayed her down as she turned and accepted her two dollars with a kiss on the hand when they were done.

"Thank you so much, Carlos," the pale redhead from England said and sighed. "Will you be giving massages later?" She eyed off his golden tanned Adonis body, licking her lips, or at least trying to, in a seductive way. All it did was make her look like the child she was.

"I'll be in the massage cabana tonight." He led her out of the tent. "Next."

"Oh, Carlos." A voluptuous Colombian woman known as Connie stepped onto the mat. "Will you save a special massage for me later?" She stood straight with her shoulders back so her large breasts were front and centre.

And they were quite delightful breasts as Carlos had found out two nights ago when she'd come for a massage and showed him exactly where and how he should massage her. And he'd massaged her all the way to an orgasm for which she'd paid extra.

"Connie, my Luv." His Aussie accent was strong this year as his grandparents had come over for a month. It was winter back in Australia and they'd wanted to see their grandchildren. Desperate for anything from back home, they'd spent so much time with each other that their old Australian speech pattern was in full force. Not that they'd ever completely picked up Greek, but it had influenced the way he and his brothers spoke. His bright blue eyes twinkled. "Do you want me to take you to heaven tonight?" He sprayed her down as she turned.

"Oh, yes, Carlos." Her Colombian accent came thick and fast as black tendrils of hair gently hung down from the riot of curls captured on top of her head. "I want you to *come* and massage me tonight. I pay well." She handed over her money. "For golden stud like you, I pay very well." She wandered off leaving him blushing furiously.

Not that a man should be blushing, but when

you're twenty-four and have the world at your feet, having older women hit on you was quite a learning curve. Especially since it was older women who'd taught him most of what he knew.

He'd sprayed down three more women and accepted their money when the dirty old perve, Leon Spenter, stepped onto the mat.

"Hello, Carlos," Leon purred.

Carlos looked at the sixty-something man in his tiny leopard swim briefs, wrinkled and sagging over-tanned skin, and grey thinning hair. "Leon, how are you today?" he asked as he sprayed, keeping his facial expression neutral.

"Oh…delightful." Leon licked his wrinkled burnt lips. "All the more for seeing you, my Greek Adonis."

"Only half Greek," Carlos reminded him, holding out his hand for the money.

Leon pretended to hand it over, but snatched his hand back. "Half Greek or not you're still an Adonis, Carlos." He eyed the hard, muscled, tanned body of Carlos Stephanopoulos; his long, swept-back golden-brown hair, bright blue eyes, kissable lips, and a light sprinkling of chest hair underneath his tank top. "Carlos." He licked his lips again. "You're spraying oil on people and yet here you are wearing clothes. Shouldn't you be shirtless too?"

Carlos sighed. The fags could be the worst, especially when they thought he swung both ways, even though he told them he didn't. However, they kept insisting he should and didn't like paying for anything until they got what they wanted out of him.

Which they didn't. So they always left disappointed. "Pay up, Leon, or don't come back," he snapped. "You're holding up the line."

Leon saw the Greek temper flare and reluctantly handed over the money. "Just having a little bit of fun, my dear, is all."

"Go have your fun somewhere else," Carlos said, waving the next person into the tent. "I have a business to run." He turned his back on Leon and kept working. *God, what is it with some of these people?* he thought and went into robot mode. He saw, he sprayed, he collected money, but now he didn't care for what he was doing and couldn't wait for the afternoon to be over. Sure his reputation for being a stud had gotten all over the island, and sure he enjoyed most of it, especially the getting paid well part, but the rest of it could be so mundane.

At five o'clock he closed the tent flaps and put up the closed sign, much to the disappointment and murmurs of the line that was still going strong with a few repeat customers. But it was knock off time. He turned off his sprayer and shut up for the night then procceded to count the day's takings. Two thousand two hundred dollars; not bad for an afternoon's work. He slipped one thousand into a bag for the resort manager, one thousand into a bag for him to take to the bank, and slipped the two hundred into his pocket. He always kept the leftovers, and there were plenty of them, but he never told the boss about them. They were the little extras he kept for himself.

It was a great life, working and living in Greece. He

worked in his father's meat shop late fall through winter and into early spring, and lived it up on the beach for the rest of the time. Six months in the shop slicing up raw meat, and six months of sunbathing and hot women wanting hot sex. It was a great life all right, and a great job. Bartending in the morning, spraying in the afternoon, and massaging all night. It was a career he'd had for the last six years since his eighteenth birthday, and it paid so well, much better than his father's shop, that he'd saved up plenty from all the extracurricular activities.

And, of course, what the tax man didn't know wouldn't hurt him. After all, what would he put on his tax form? Sex worker? Prostitute? Lover? Fighter? Resort worker and butcher shop assistant were all he put. The tax man didn't need to know anything else.

Carlos made it home by five-thirty for a shower and a change of clothes. Pedro and Tomas, his brothers, were already there doing the same thing, and all were waiting for their father to get home from the shop.

"Hey, Mama." After kissing his mother on the cheek, he popped a cherry tomato from the salad on the kitchen counter into his mouth. "Grandma." Bending down to kiss her at the table, he asked, "So, what did you guys do today?" before sitting down himself.

Pedro came into the kitchen in his usual white pants and tank, having slept all day after working all night. He was four years younger than Carlos and had the best of both heritages; sharp blue eyes from their mother, and jet-black hair from their father. A lethal combination on a well-muscled young stud and all the girls knew it. So did Pedro.

"Is dinner nearly ready?" Pedro asked high-fiving Carlos and then kissing his mother and grandmother.

"Just waiting for your father," Jenny replied, checking the lamb in the oven.

Pedro grabbed a bottle of beer from the fridge. "Carlos, want one?"

Carlos looked in his brother's direction. "Yeah."

Pedro got out two and handed one over before sitting down next to him on their side of the table. Whenever there were guests, the boys all sat on one side of the table while the guests had the other.

Tomas strolled in from his shower and joined them. The middle son, he looked just like their father; tall, lean, but well-muscled, with jet-black hair, piercing black eyes, and a spread of jet-black hair across his well-toned chest that trailed down to his navel. He was also the quiet one in the family.

"My, how you all look so much like your parents," their grandmother, Sarah, said.

At that moment Spiros Stephanopoulos walked through the door carrying half a frozen lamb on his shoulder. "Is there room in the freezer?" he asked Jenny before walking down the hall into the laundry slash extra kitchen where they had a small walk-in freezer. He'd installed it when he took over the family business and they'd moved into his parents' house. He dumped the lamb on a shelf and walked back into the kitchen. Everyone looked at him in disdain. "What?" He looked down and saw his apron and clothes were meat- and blood-soaked.

"There is no way you're sitting down to dinner like that." Jenny pushed him toward the bedroom. "Go take a shower, dinner's nearly ready."

With a cheeky flick of his wife's behind and a wink to his three manly sons, Spiros went to shower. He was still a fine-looking man at the age of fifty-two, and at fifty-two he still couldn't believe how lucky he was to have met such an amazing woman in Jenny. And still he couldn't believe she'd taken a chance on him; the immigrant Greek boy who'd sailed the seas in 1950 to a little country on the other side of the world known as Australia.

He'd landed in Sydney by himself, being the only one in his family to make the trip to a new promised land, and had met her within minutes as she was one of the helpers at the dock directing strangers to the places they needed to go. And it had been easy to direct him as the distant relatives he was staying with lived right next door to her.

Over the next year, she had taught him English and fallen in love with him, accepted his marriage proposal, and married him after he'd set himself up in a butcher's shop. Meat was all he knew; having grown up in his father's butcher shop, and so he quickly took over this new one, becoming the manager within a year which was good because Jenny gave birth to Carlos and the extra money was helpful.

He was also eternally grateful that she had agreed to move halfway around the world when his father died. It meant he needed to take over the family business and Jenny had urged him to go. Now, here they were ten years after moving back, and she still stuck it out with him, and he made it up to her every year by inviting her family members to stay for the summer. It also helped the boys keep in touch with their Australian roots.

Spiros quickly dried off and dressed, making it to the table just as the lamb came out of the oven. "Smells good." He watched Jenny place the pan in front of him and carved it up. "Let's eat."

They ate in silence for a few minutes before getting into a review of the day.

"You boys have a good day at work?" Jenny asked.

Carlos and Pedro exchanged wicked grins, but Tomas just sat quietly.

"Absolutely," Carlos said. "This resort thing is paying well."

"Better than the shop?" Spiros asked, spearing a piece of lamb with his fork.

All three boys glanced at him. This routine was nothing new. He asked every time their mother did, and they answered the same way every time.

"Yes, Papa, it pays better," Carlos replied.

"Much better," Pedro added. He was becoming a bit of a stud in his own right, and was earning as much money DJing four nights a week on Santorini as he figured Carlos did at the resort.

"Well, I hope you're saving that money for your own home one day," Spiros went on. "And not wasting it on frivolous things like women." He knew his sons had his Greek blood in them, and the stories that made it back to him made his hair curlier than it already was. Especially the stories about Carlos. Although, he was secretly proud of having a stud for a son, the things he heard he could sometimes do without hearing.

"Yes, Papa." Carlos and Pedro knew not to wind him up as he had a temper when the need arose.

"Good. You'll be able to look after your parents when they're old then." Spiros grinned wickedly, the same grin his sons had.

The boys rolled their eyes.

"In your dreams," Pedro said. "I've got my life to live and the rest of it to pay for. I need all the money I can get. Carlos can look after you, he's the oldest."

"Geez, thanks," Carlos drawled and finished off his beer.

They chatted their way through dessert and then the boys left for their night shifts. All three worked hard. While Pedro did only night shifts, it was still a gruelling eight to twelve hours long. Carlos and Tomas worked all day and then worked a night shift until midnight.

Mykonos was great that way. People swam and sunbaked all day while the sun was up, but when the sun went down all they wanted to do was party. Money flowed, beer flowed, drugs flowed, sex flowed, and Carlos was off to the resort to be masseur for the night and make sure the sex and money kept on flowing.

He strolled into the cabana to find Gary, the hot young Australian, finishing off for the day.

"Glad ya made it, mate," he said with a flick of his blond locks. "I'm pooped, gonna have a drink and hit the sack."

"With a woman?" Carlos got a pile of towels ready.

"Or a man." Gary winked and strode off into the night, all six foot five and tanned and ready for anything.

"Oh, Carlos," Connie sang through the curtain.

"I'm not open yet, Connie, you'll have to wait a few minutes." He laid out the new sheet on the bed.

"Well, *I am* open Carlos and ready to be massaged by your long, strong…fingers…"

Carlos frowned and grinned at the same time. As much as he loved getting paid for his job, and loved bedding women each and every night, sometimes it was a bit overbearing.

"You'll just have to wait, Connie." He spread rose petals on the bed, lit candles, and made sure the thick curtains were closed. He couldn't have people catching him in the act of servicing all of these women or he'd be out on his rear.

Checking his watch he let Connie in, marking her off the booking sheet. Every massage had to be booked in so they knew how long for each, and so customers weren't just waiting at the curtain ready to come in. That's why the cabana was in a private area of the resort, only frequented by guests when they were let in. Few staff came and went, so Carlos had not been caught.

Yet.

He closed the curtains after checking to see if anyone was around and found Connie naked on the bed. "Connie," he admonished. "You know we start off slow and build up to the crescendo."

"Oh, I know." She bent her knees and spread her legs. "But I've been waiting for you all day."

He stood between her legs and closed them. "On your stomach first."

She groaned. "Do I have to?" The Colombian woman was full in every sense, from her voluptuous bosoms to her voluptuous thatch, curved hips, strong thighs, and an even stronger vagina.

Clearly, she did her Kegels every day.

"On yer stomach," Carlos said and crossed his arms. "Time's money and you're wasting precious moments."

Connie quickly rolled over, and Carlos mounted the table, sitting on her ass to massage her shoulders.

"Oh…Carlos…" She groaned, gripping the sides of the table.

He slowly ran his fingers up her spine and across her shoulders to loosen the muscles, doing this for several minutes before making his way down her legs until he was standing at the end of the table, massaging her calves, her ankles, her feet, hitting the pressure spots of pleasure.

"Oh, God, Carlos, take me, fuck me."

Carlos knew she was ready, and so was he. Pushing down his shorts, he set his erection free and allowed it solace in the one spot it awaited. Snapping on a condom, he grabbed Connie by the ankles, yanked her down the table until her lower half was barely hanging off the bed, and proceeded to fill her aching soul.

"Oh, Carlos, oh, God yes," she groaned, burying her head in the bed and grasping the sides of it until her knuckles went white.

His hands continued their massage, his penis joined in. Up her spine his fingers went while he matched the movement inside her. Down his fingers came to her backside as he withdrew. Up her spine again, and down her spine again. Over and over.

"Oh, God, Carlos, now, now oh, God now," Connie panted.

His thrusts became fast and furious, grunting into her until he was done and she was screaming his name.

They collapsed on the table, still entwined, but Carlos soon pulled out and cleaned up. Sweat trickled down his face and he pushed his hair back.

"Oh, Carlos…"

He turned to see Connie sitting on the end of the bed.

"Come, my darling." Her arms were outstretched and her bosoms inviting. Carlos was enveloped into her embrace as she pushed his tank top over his head and let it fall to the floor. His shorts followed. She pulled him close and rubbed herself over him. The feel of his hot Adonis body against her no longer youthful one felt refreshing. Her breasts remained hardened against his chest, and his hard-on came back. "Carlos, oh, Carlos," she whispered. "Take me, take me again."

He took her on the edge of the table, with hard grunting thrusts until he was done and she was on her back, remaining inside as she grabbed his hands and placed them on her breasts.

"Squeeze." He squeezed. So did she and he hardened again. "Squeeze."

They played the game until they both came and both stopped squeezing.

"No more." Carlos stumbled back, panting. He was done, and she was only his first customer. Checking his watch, he saw her time was up and quickly dressed, saying, "Time to go, Connie," before brushing his hair back.

"Go, Carlos? Oh, no, I'm not going anywhere. I've booked you out for the whole night. Come to me, Carlos, let's see if you have the stamina to please Constance DeLuca all night. If you can, there is big money in it for you."

Looking at her open arms and open legs he cocked a brow. "Big money?"

"*Very* big money."

He stripped off. "All right then."

*****

Carlos could barely walk the next morning when he turned up for bartending duties.

"Whoa, dude," Antonio said when he spied Carlos. "What happened to you?" He finished making the drink and handed it over to the sexy young thing at the bar.

She winked and waved her fingers at Antonio and then saw Carlos. Her eyes went wide and she stopped sipping her drink which was just as well since she wasn't looking where she was going due to her attention being diverted to the hot bartender that had just arrived. She tripped, her face went into shock, and she fell face first into the sand.

"Oops." Antonio raced around the bar to help her

to her feet. "Are you all right, miss?" Antonio picked up the glass once she was standing.

"Oh," she cried in a British accent. "I feel so stupid."

"No, no," Antonio soothed. "Women lose their mind when they see Carlos. I'll get you another drink." He helped her to a bar stool and quickly made another margarita. Taking it back to her, he saw her eyeing Carlos off who was serving another customer. "Here you go…ma'am."

She finally noticed he was there and blushed. "Oh, I'm sorry. I didn't see you…" Accepting the drink her eyes travelled up and down his muscular frame.

"Most women don't," Antonio replied dryly.

"How much?" she asked.

"For what? Carlos?"

She blushed harder. "The drink."

"Oh." Now it was Antonio's turn to blush. "It's on the house. Since you had an accident and all."

"Oh." The redness deepened and her eyes became hooded. "Thank you."

"Welcome."

"I'll just…" She moved and pointed to her friends who all stood wide-eyed and giggling.

"Right." Antonio smiled and waved at her friends whose eyes grew wider and they all blushed.

"Um, thanks."

"No problems."

"Um, bye."

"Bye."

"I'll just…" She backed away from him only to nearly trip again.

"Whoa, careful." Antonio grabbed her before she could fall.

"Oh, um, thanks…" Gazing up at him knowing she was beet red, she felt dizzy. Dizzy over this manly man touching her.

"That's okay. Don't forget sunscreen."

"What?"

"You're red." He waved a finger at her wavy hair. "You don't want to burn in this hot, heady Greek sun." If he played his cards right, he might score with this girl by the end of the day. It's not like Carlos should have all the fun. Right?

"Um, thanks, I'll put it on." She reluctantly turned, and with a wave walked over to her friends who all started teasing her about the hot bartender helping her.

Antonio waved to all of them and got back to work. It was not as if he wasn't good looking. He was the son of Spanish and Colombian parents, so was full of brooding dark good looks and hot and spicy personality. He'd had no complaints in the bed department either, but when Carlos was around, he got fewer women perving at him and more women asking for Carlos's phone number. He felt like a dud next to the Greek god, even though he, Antonio Stephano DeLuca, had been the stud in his high school and college. Growing up half Spanish, half Colombian and being raised in Spain, he'd been celebrated for being his father's son and for being so damned gorgeous. Now, here, he seemed to be a nobody. Even though his father was big time bullfighter Stephano DeLuca, name dropping got him nowhere. Especially on the Greek islands every summer where he came to work while his mother played it up.

Yes, he knew his parents had an open marriage, but that didn't mean he had to like it. After all, they were both in their fifties, but sick of each other and of having sex with the same partner all the time. That's why they had lovers on the side. It was a fact Antonio tried to forget.

He made it back to the bar. "Did you see that little hottie? I think she's into me." He picked up a towel and wiped down the bar, gazing in the direction of the girls who he noticed occasionally looked back.

"Could be, man." Carlos served up two beers and three margaritas. "She certainly noticed you *after* she fell over."

Antonio smirked. "Are you saying she didn't notice me before that?"

Carlos grinned back. "You did see her looking at me, right?"

"Nah, man. She wasn't looking at you at all," Antonio joked. There was an edge to his voice because quite frankly, he was sick of not getting any attention when Carlos was around. It's as if he was suddenly invisible and the only man on the planet was Carlos. "So, what's with the weird walk this morning? Hard night was it?"

Carlos thought back. Connie had worked him hard all night and paid him handsomely for it. Ten thousand dollars for four hours work. All cash under the table. She'd told him he was worth it; he'd grinned and hidden the money in his private stash when he'd gotten home. "Yeah, man, I was hard all night. Got worked real hard." He cracked open a bottle of champagne and poured five glasses.

"By some hot young thing?" Antonio didn't particularly care for Carlos's exploits, but a part of him always wanted to know the gritty details just to see whether he was missing out on any pussy that was in town.

"Nah, man, your mother!" Carlos joked and pulled out more glasses from under the counter.

Antonio blinked. "You screwed my mother?"

Carlos glanced over at him and saw his expression. "Joke, dude!"

Antonio blinked again. "Oh, right. Coz you know, my mother actually *is* in town."

Carlos stopped what he was doing. *"Your mother's in town?"*

"Yeah." Antonio served up a wine. "Constance Philomena Stephanova Constinopolous DeLuca. I'd be surprised if you haven't met her already."

"Connie?" Carlos stopped dead. *"Connie's your mother?"*

*****

"Oh, darling, I have found the perfect stud. He is pleasing all of my needs and does it to me almost every night." Connie DeLuca spoke down the line to her friend Harriet DeVille in L.A.

Harriet was the wife of bigwig porno producer Harry DeVille, and everyone always joked about them being Harry and Harriet. "How big is he?" she asked.

"Big enough to fill me ten times over," Connie replied.

"But how…*big…is he?*"

"Oh, you mean cock size? About ten inches."

Harriet drew a breath. "And what does the rest of him look like?"

"Five-foot-ten, long golden-brown hair, blue eyes, golden-brown tan, muscles from here to there…"

"Would he be good enough for us?"

"Oh, darling, he'd be good enough for everyone."

"Well, maybe I should fly out there and take a look?"

Connie bristled. No one was taking her man while she was in town. "No, no, darling, he is much too busy. You stay and deal with your business, but if he's ever out your way, I'll recommend you."

There was silence.

"Are you trying to keep him all to yourself, Connie?"

"He's hardly all mine," Connie replied. "I don't think I'm the only one he services."

"Is he using protection?"

"Of course."

"At least he has the brains to do that."

"And the head!"

They laughed.

*****

Antonio looked at Carlos in surprise. "Yeah, that's what people call her, why?" He didn't like what his gut was telling him.

Carlos tried not to let his panic show. "Uh, there's a Connie that comes for a spray every afternoon…oil spray…average height, black curls piled on her head, accent, big…" He held his hands in front of his chest. "Ah…" His hands lowered.

Antonio raised a brow. "Yeah, that's my mother." He stepped towards Carlos and poked his chest. "And *you* stay away from her."

Carlos put his hands up in defeat and backed away. "I've not gone near her," he lied, which he had gotten quite good at doing after all the years of being a lothario. "Just oil spray man, nothing else." He watched Antonio back away and turned around. Taking a deep breath, he quietly let it out and got back to work. He'd need to be careful from now on.

*****

That night, as he was massaging the back of a thirty-something starlet, Carlos thought back to Connie and Antonio. There was no way he could ever find out, and he'd already warned Connie that afternoon when she'd come for her spray.

"He knows we know each other," he'd said.

"Who knows?" She'd delighted in his presence.

"Antonio, your son. I work with him," Carlos had said angrily in low tones. "I didn't know you two were related and thank God I never mentioned this to anyone."

"You work with Antonio here at the resort?" Her eyes had mischievously twinkled. "I didn't know he

worked at this one. I knew he was somewhere on the islands. Well, what do you know? You work with him every day, and you work me over every night."

"It's not funny," he'd hissed. *"If he finds out it could get ugly."*

"He won't." Connie winked and walked away.

He'd fumed about it for the rest of the day and now found himself giving massages once again.

"Is something wrong?"

He blinked and refocussed on the blonde woman before him. "What?"

She was now on her side, posing, one leg bent and moving back and forth to show off the Brazilian wax job she'd had done earlier.

He didn't like them clean, maybe that was the Greek in him, but he preferred his women with bush. Somehow it made them seem like women instead of the pre-pubescent girls they were trying to be.

"Am I distracting you?" The Hollywood star, to whom he couldn't put a name, flicked her long blonde tendrils over her right shoulder and rubbed her nipple.

It turned him off. He wasn't sure why. Maybe her lack of thatch, maybe it was just that the same monotonous women all looked the same. Thin, white, blonde, or sometimes red or brunette, or both, or all three. He preferred exotic sexy types that got his blood racing.

She sat up in front of him and slid to her feet. "Because *you're* distracting *me*." She slid her fingers over his broad chest and muscular arms before sliding them into his shorts.

He stopped her short with his hand and his piercing gaze. "That will be extra."

She gazed up into those big blue eyes that penetrated into her soul. Her gut clenched and danced the tango. Her womanhood had been moist since she first laid eyes on him. "How much?"

"One thousand for a quick fuck, two thousand for the hour. All cash, all under the table and off the books."

She glanced at the delicate gold watch on her left wrist. "Just as well I booked two hours; you have an hour and a half left. That's three thousand dollars." She pushed his top up and slid her tongue down his tanned torso. Going to her knees, her mouth went to his erection as she pulled down his pants. She knew how to please a man, had been taught from an early age by her stepdaddy and had every man begging for more. But this one was different. He didn't want her. She sensed that, and that made it all the more of a rush. Controlling a man that didn't want her. She took him inside all the way, what was known as deep-throating him.

He groaned, how could he not. It wasn't often he got sucked and when he did, if it was good; he enjoyed it immensely.

She licked, sucked and swallowed, getting to her feet when she was finished. "You want me now, don't you?"

He picked her up, threw her on the table, hitched her legs over his shoulders and showed her how much.

*****

"Carlos," the blonde bimbo from Australia called across the bar. "When are we going to get together again?"

He barely recognised her as his lunchtime conquest from several days previous and couldn't even come up with a name. "And why would we get together again? Once was more than enough." He handed a jug of beer to a customer.

The blonde went red. *"What do you mean once was enough?"* she yelled. "You don't get to fuck me at lunchtime, and then go back to work and not see me again." She stood with her hands on her hips, her legs spread, and her face was as red as her teeny tiny almost non-existent bright red bikini.

The crowd went silent. Their eyes flitted back and forth from the furious Barbie doll to the tanned Adonis. It was like a tennis match of mass proportions.

"You don't get to fuck me and leave me, Carlos. You don't get to seduce me into your bed and then leave me like a piece of…of…" She looked around for a word to use.

"Crap?" someone offered.

"Yeah, crap," she said.

Carlos sighed. This wasn't the first time he'd dealt with an airhead like her; he'd dealt with several since summer started and wondered why he kept getting involved with the same type. He had to play it cool and polite, so put down the glass he was wiping. "I'm sorry," he said, leaning on the bar. "I'm sorry if I gave you the wrong impression. I live and work here, *you're* a tourist. I told you it wasn't anything other than a quick fuck and you said okay. And now you're saying

I've done *you* wrong. Well, I'm sorry you see it that way when I was never anything other than truthful."

"Of course you told me that." She reddened, well aware of the crowd staring at her. And it was getting to her. "But I thought it would be different. *You* would be different."

"If he told you the truth you didn't have the right to expect anything more," an older woman in a black one-piece said. Her face was hidden by her large sunhat and even larger black sunglasses. "And now you're here attacking him in front of everyone when *you* are the one in the wrong. He told you how it was; you were the one dumb enough to expect more. You don't get it both ways, sweetheart." The woman walked up to the bar. "Vodka martini, two olives, dry."

But Barbie kept fuming. "And *who are you* to tell me I'm wrong and dumb?" She marched over to the woman and ripped her hat off.

Luscious brunette waves tumbled down her back and the woman oh so casually turned to the girl and removed her glasses.

Everyone gasped, and the little blonde bimbo stammered, "Oh, my, oh, I'm so sorry, Ms Villiers."

Vivian Villiers was one of the hottest supermodels in the world, and even at forty she still knocked them dead with her killer body and even deadlier smile. Her hair swayed against her ripe, firm ass, and her breasts were still natural, high, and well-rounded. She hadn't had any children, so her body was kept in shape by two hours a day of Pilates, yoga, and swimming. Plus, she drank more than she ate. Food that is. Whereas she ate men for breakfast, lunch *and* dinner.

"My hat?" Vivian held out her hand. "And *I* am a woman, a *real* woman, who knows an immature, insecure little brat who doesn't get her own way when I see one."

Barbie went deep red and handed over the hat.

"Thank you. *Now,* he told you the truth but you refused to accept it. *Grow up and move on.* I'm sure he's not the only one who's been dipping into that pool." She waved her off. "Run along, little girl."

The blonde finally moved, moved into a run, and then a sprint as she tried to get as far away from the humiliation as possible. The laughter behind her echoed in her ear until she ran all the way back to her small apartment she shared with her friends. She threw herself on the bed and then just as quickly jumped off. That was where they'd fucked, and where he'd left her, never to return. Oh, no, Carlos Spiros Stephanopoulos was not going to do this to her. Not to Barbara Weston, the girl he'd so unceremoniously dumped in high school and then ignored. He was *not* going to fuck her and leave her. Oh, no, he was going to be taught a lesson. And teach him, she would.

✳✳✳✳✳

Vivian Villiers wound her hair up into a bun and covered it with her hat. Replacing her sunglasses, she took her seat at the bar and waved off the admirers that had gathered round. "Please, please, I'm here incognito, and you wouldn't even know it was me if that girl hadn't ripped my hat off. Please, let me have my privacy to drink my martini." She turned her back and sat facing the bar, facing the extremely popular Carlos Stephanopoulos whom she'd heard about from her friend, Harriet DeVille. She'd been on Santorini for the last month, but after hearing about the stud at the resort had booked a room and made her way over by ferry. She crossed her long creamy legs and sipped her drink, watching Carlos as Carlos watched her.

He was serving the other guests, but kept glancing at the supermodel at his bar. The gorgeous Viv as she was known, the one he'd had wet dreams about since he was fourteen-years-old, was sitting at *his* bar sipping *his* martini. He was flushed. Flushed with adrenaline at the woman of his dreams sitting there, eyeing him off. He hardened and was excited that she might be one of his conquests.

"Hey, Carlos, time for lunch, my man." Antonio came over and Carlos took off. He didn't know where he was going, just that he needed to get out of there to relieve his hard-on. Having made his way to the massage cabana that was free for a couple of hours at lunchtime, he pulled out his erection to let it run free.

A hand grabbed it from behind.

A female hand.

Carlos turned to see Vivian Villiers behind him.

"Let me," she rasped and stepped out of her black one-piece in one fluid motion.

He grabbed a condom and had her on the table in seconds, entering her before she had time to wrap her legs around him.

"Oh, ugh, God," she groaned at every hard thrust. She locked her fingers into his golden locks and locked her legs together to keep him in.

Hard motions sent *him* forward and *her* over the edge. Coming to a stop he collapsed on top of her, resting his head in his hand, looking down at the dewy complexion made moist by his thrusting, the shy smile made soft by his coming, and the lips so ripe for the kissing. His fingers gently rubbed her face, his hand taking it within his grasp. He kissed her, soft and slow with just a little bit of tongue.

But she wanted so much more and took his tongue fiercely into her mouth. The kiss was as passionate as the sex and barely came to a stop.

"Oh, Carlos," she sighed. "You're as good as they say."

That intrigued him. "As who say?"

"Harriet DeVille."

"Who's she?"

"A friend of Constance DeLuca. Connie told Harriet, Harriet told me."

"Wait." He sat up. "You only wanted me because you've heard about my exploits?" He wasn't sure how he felt about being talked about by a bunch of horny old women.

Viv sat up beside him. "Oh, I've heard." She stroked his penis, making it harden. "You're a very attractive young man, Carlos, and have a lot to offer a woman in that department."

He gazed into her emerald cat-shaped eyes. They were the most striking thing about her. "Yeah, well, you got a freebie." He started to get off the massage table, but her hand on his arm stopped him.

"And that's why I booked you all night for a massage."

He gazed at the beauty before him. Somehow having her pay him made him feel dirty. "Normally I charge two thousand an hour for extracurricular activities, but tonight I'll meet you in your room instead."

"In my room?" She stroked his lips with her tongue, thinking how tasty they were.

"Your room," he said, stroking back. "Because I've dreamt about you since I was fourteen and there's no way I'm going to use my fantasy to fuck you like an animal. Tonight, I'm going to make love to you, all night, and make both of our dreams come true."

*****

"Carlos Spiros Stephanopoulos get back here right now."

Carlos heard his father's yell as he ran into his room. He'd been held back at work and arrived home with only half an hour till his next shift. A shift he couldn't wait to get to. He dumped his bag and ran back to the lounge room. "Papa, I've got half an hour, I need a shower."

"Work can wait. Sit down," his father ordered.

"But Pa—"

"Sit!" Spiros raged.

Carlos knew better than to push it once fire spat from his father's eyes, because all three boys knew not to interrupt their parents when a brother was being chastised. He sat on the sofa. "What? What now?"

Jenny sat beside her husband. "A young girl came to us today Carlos and told us a story. A story about what you did to her."

Uh oh, he thought, *better play it cool.* "What girl?"

"A young girl by the name of Barbara Weston came to me today and told me, in tears mind you, how you had taken advantage of her."

Carlos raised a brow. "Believe me; I *do not* take advantage of anyone."

"What she told us disgusted us, Carlos, so listen," Spiros said. He sat steely-eyed and determined. No son of his was going to take advantage of a young girl. He had raised them better.

Carlos sighed. "Who's Barbara Weston?"

"Carlos," his mother admonished. "Don't you remember the young Australian girl you slept with over a month ago and then discarded like an old shoe? Do you *really* not remember her?"

He shook his head. "Name doesn't ring a bell. Describe her."

"Young, about your age, long blonde hair, big blue eyes, slim, very pretty."

He frowned at the description. "She *sounds* familiar, but only because I saw her *two days* ago, *not* a month ago. And I certainly didn't take advantage of her, or anyone else for that matter." He stood. "Is that it? Some girl makes up a story because she's outsmarted by a supermodel and now she's blabbing that story to my parents? I'm outta here."

"Sit down," Spiros roared. "You do not get away

with shirking your responsibilities. Now, I don't know what you're talking about, but you will do the right thing by this young girl and your baby."

Baby!

"Baby? What baby?" Carlos slumped to his seat. "How can she be pregnant in two days? I used protection."

"What do you mean in two days?" Jenny asked. "You were with her over a month ago." She couldn't keep up with her sons anymore.

"Mama, Papa, I only slept with this girl *two days ago.*" Carlos was on his feet again. "I *used* a condom. She *can't* be pregnant by me, ah-uh, no way." He waved his hand. "And if she is, it *ain't* mine. She came to the bar this morning and bitched about me in front of everyone. I told her I had been up front about sleeping with her and didn't want anything else out of it. *She* apparently did and tried to confront me about it. She only got stopped when Vivian Villiers, *the supermodel,* told her to grow up and get over it. That she was acting like an immature brat. She got embarrassed and ran away. *That's it.* If she's pregnant, *it ain't mine.* Now," he looked at his watch, "I'm gonna be late for my shift and I gotta shower." He left his parents speechless, unsure of who was telling the truth.

"Vivian Villiers," Jenny muttered. "She's here? She's gorgeous."

"And probably embarrassed the poor girl," Spiros replied. "Do you think it may be some revenge thing?"

"What?" Jenny said. "Carlos sleeps with her once and she gets told off by a supermodel and then plans revenge on him? No, I think that would be a bit too much for her to handle."

"Ah, never underestimate a woman scorned," Spiros said, nodding in agreement with himself.

*****

Carlos raced to the cabana and arrived at the same time as Vivian. "Ah," he gasped. "Made it."

"But look at you," she purred. "You're all hot…and sweaty…" She pulled at his tank top.

"And you're all naked under that robe, aren't you," he said, his chest heaving from more than exertion.

"Yes." The wicked grin slid into place.

"Well, we'd better get to it then. I suggest we go to your place." Carlos grabbed her hand. "I know a private entrance. What room are you in?"

"I don't want to go back up." She pulled him to her. "I came down here for some privacy and alone time."

"You may have," Carlos said. "But there's no way I'm making love to you on a massage table, so your bedroom it is." He pulled her to the back entrance of the hotel and they made their way up the private stairs that all of the celebrities used to stay away from the paps, making it to her room without being seen. She locked the door, he yanked off her robe, and she ripped his clothes off.

They stood before the bed facing each other and each admiring the other's body. He grabbed her head, entangling his hand in her hair. She did the same. He bent her head back and kissed her roughly, his other arm holding her tight. After moments of passionate tongue sex, he lifted her and she wrapped her legs around him before they fell onto the bed as one.

After hours of vigorous, seductive and languid lovemaking they lay spent in each other's arms.

Carlos held her tight. He didn't want to let his dream woman go. He relished the tendrils of hair that lay across his naked body and twirled them around his finger. They had been a silken cascade that she flung around her in a frenzy during sex, allowing it to tease him, torment him. Now, he held her against him.

Viv sighed, contented. She hadn't had a man like that in a long time, let alone one nearly half her age. Some would see him still a boy, but he'd just proved he was definitely all man. A young, very virile, man. She ran her fingers down his chest. "You *are* good," she purred. "Probably the best I've ever had."

"Only probably?" he murmured into her hair.

The tropical island breeze floated through the open balcony doors. Three empty bottles of champagne lay strewn across the floor. They had made use of every part of the room. The chairs, desk, bathroom, bed, the floor...

She twirled her fingers around. "Well...I'd say... *definitely.*"

"That's more like it."

Her fingers trailed their way down to his manhood and gently massaged it.

"Ugh...yeah...that's..." He arched his back and sighed.

"I know how to please a man, you know," she said, sitting on top of him.

"Ugh." He grabbed her hips and kept her there, gazing up into her fiery eyes. She came, throwing her head back at the peak, and he sat, making it more explosive. He buried his mouth in her hair, his tongue seeking nipple. His hands moved up to claim them and found them, making them his own.

She sighed and fell beside him. "You really are everything they say you are. You should do it for a living."

"Do what?"

"Have sex."

"I already do."

"But I mean on the big screen." She sat up so they were nose to nose. "Imagine it. Your gorgeous body, that ten inch cock." She stroked it. "All on the big screen. All for everyone to see. The world will want you, just like I do," she said against his lips.

"You mean movies?"

"More than movies."

"What could be more than movies?"

"Pornos, darling. Let the world see what a massive dick you've got."

Carlos laughed and pushed her off him. "Pornos?" Getting out of bed he checked his watch. He was now off the clock. Grabbing his clothes, he said, "Me? In pornos? Movies yeah, but pornos?"

"Have you ever thought about it?" Viv asked, yanking his clothes from his grasp. She knelt on the bed in front of him. "Look at you." He stood before her in the raw. "You're beautiful. The dream guy every girl wants. Sure, you could go to Hollywood and *try* and get into movies. I could help you if you wanted. But for a man with a cock that long and that wide and that…" She groped it, kneaded it, massaged it until he came in her hand and groaned. "Pleasurable," she added. "You need to show it off. Besides, you can earn big bucks on the big screen just for having a big dick." She slid her hand between her legs, feeling the warm juice over her. "Think about it. I can help you."

*****

Consuela Maria Da Vica was preparing for her wedding. She was a young thing, barely twenty-five years old and already considered past her prime, age-wise. But she was still young enough to bear big strong children. She was preparing to marry an older man, as old as her grandfather, purely as breeding stock. Her parents had wanted her out of their home, crying poor when he came along.

He had taken a shine to her and asked for her hand in marriage, paying her parents handsomely. They had packed up her meagre belongings and sent her on her way with her new husband-to-be. She had objected at first. She didn't know him, he needed to court her. But between him and her parents, she was out of her small Peruvian town in no time.

Now, here she was in the beautiful Greek city of Athens, ensconced in her husband-to-be's palatial home. She knew no one, knew nothing, and felt like a prisoner half the time. She wasn't allowed to go anywhere without a bodyguard and servant, a young maid who was the daughter of the cook, and who she was sure was being eyed off by her husband-to-be. And she also had a feeling that he'd given it to the cook over the years.

Consuela spoke broken English, but now had to learn Greek. Not that it mattered, as she was sure she would never be out in public with her husband. She knew she was just for breeding. And here it was, one week before the wedding, three weeks since she'd been brought there, and all that had to be done was get a dress. From a catalogue, she had chosen a simple design which they were having shipped in from the company.

She wandered over to the large balcony doors and stared out at the city. "Oh, what will become of me? Besides a breeder. Will I ever work or play or have fun again?" She'd had so much fun in her small town. Her best friend was married off with children. But she hadn't wanted to be married off herself. She'd wanted to see the world and go to places she'd only ever heard of. Now she was. She was seeing Athens and new and exciting things. Even though it was only because she was being married off.

Her maid came into the room. "Madame." Her broken English was hesitant. "What do you want to do today?" She hovered behind her new mistress. *She's such a young thing*, she thought. *Barely older than me. I wonder if she knows she's marrying my father? I'll kill her…*flew through her mind before she smoothed her apron.

"I do not know," Consuela managed. "I am not allowed out of this house. I cannot do anything."

The maid, whose name was Marta Effidopolous, had already concocted a plan. "I know," she said. Glancing behind her she moved to Consuela's side. "We will go to Mykonos."

"What's Mykonos?" Consuela asked.

Marta's eyes widened at the girl's stupidity. "It is in Greek islands. We can take ferry there. We can go get some sun, have fun. I can dress you in maid's outfit, no one will ever know. We will be gone and back."

Consuela fretted. "It sounds good, but how and when?" The thought of getting out into the air thrilled her, even if it was dangerous.

"Leave it to me," Marta said. "Boss man is leaving Friday for business and not coming back until Monday. We can leave straight after."

The more Consuela thought about it, the more excited she became. "Okay, let's do it." Little did she know what she was in for.

*****

The next few days flew by, with Carlos bedding Vivian more often than not, pleading innocent to his parents, and demanding the Aussie bimbo get a pregnancy test, plus staying away from Connie, his second most voracious customer. When finding out he was servicing Viv, Connie more than offered to join in. He declined. She was annoyed.

*****

The time flew by for Consuela as well. Marta had given her a uniform to wear, and they packed small bags to take with them. Marta let Gustoff, Consuela's bodyguard, in on her plan, making him promise not to say anything to their boss. He agreed. Marta thanked him and told Consuela she could trust him to not say anything, but they needed him to get them to the wharf so they could travel.

Consuela baulked. "Why would you tell him? It must be secret."

"He is my fiancé," Marta lied. "He will help us. Don't worry."

Consuela was so ecstatic about going and so naïve and young, she didn't even know it was a lie.

*****

On Friday morning, after Consuela's husband-to-be had left, Marta, Gustoff, and Consuela made their way to the car. Consuela was in one of Marta's uniforms and had her hair under the cap. They made it past the guard and out to the ferry with no problem. Four hours later they arrived on Mykonos.

Consuela was astounded. "It is so beautiful," she said.

"Come." Marta pulled her along. "I have booked hotel rooms for us."

They made their way to their hotel, checked in, and found the two bedroom suite to be to their liking. It had views of the beach, was a quick ride to town, and had a private cabana for massages.

*****

Carlos finished up at the bar for the day and made his way to Vivian's room. He'd become addicted to her, no doubt about it, and had stopped seeing other women since being with her. Even Connie. And Barbara had disappeared after being threatened with a lawsuit by his father. If she couldn't prove she was having his grandchild, she could go back to where she'd come from.

Viv opened the door then opened her legs. They barely made it to the bed before joining. When they were done, they drank from the same bottle of champagne and ate oysters and caviar, then made love before he had to leave.

"Are you coming tonight?" she asked as he dressed to leave.

A cocky grin covered his face. "I come every night."

"And then some," she added, sucking on the bottle of champagne to show how far she could deep-throat it.

It turned him on, and it showed as he turned for her to take him into her mouth and do the same to him. "Ugh… Can't… Tonight… Working…ugh…" Giddiness washed over him and he felt limp.

"Just massages?" she inquired, wiping him off her lips.

"Just…massages…" he replied, shoving it back in his pants.

*****

Marta took Consuela on a trip around Mykonos; the town, the beaches, the windmills.

Consuela revelled in the freedom, sitting on the beach at sundown, letting the sun warm her face. She breathed deeply. The salty air of the islands was exactly what she needed, and she thanked God for Marta, although, she wasn't sure about Gustoff and whether she could trust him. He did, after all, work for her future husband.

Marta found her on the beach. "I have us booked in for massages. I am at seven, you are eight. I will go first."

"Massages?" Consuela panicked. "I have never had massage. What happens? What do I do? What do *they* do?"

Marta laughed. "It is nothing to worry about. You lie on bed and get muscles massaged. You will feel nice and loose when done. It is for eight o'clock in cabana at back of hotel. Be there." She wandered off and made her way to the cabana for her own massage. *Silly little bitch,* she thought, *she has no idea.* Marta found him waiting for her when she got there and was startled. "You are gorgeous," she murmured at the Greek Adonis before her.

"So I've been told," he quipped. "Why don't you lie face down on the bed?" He motioned to the white sheet and rose petal covered table, and she disrobed down to her bikini.

She hardly wore one back in Athens so rarely got to show off her body. It wasn't bad, as she was in good shape and worked regularly on her tan. Her breasts were medium-sized and still sat high. Her bottom was a little too big, but apparently, some men liked big-assed girls. She lay face down on the table, and Carlos got to work. Within minutes he had her groaning. "Oh, God, that is good…good…oh, God."

He pushed his fingers into her back muscles, working them, kneading them up and down her spine. "You're very stiff," he said. "Do you do a lot of bending?"

She thought of all the times she'd bent to service a man. "Yes."

"It shows." Carlos moved onto her shoulders. "Same here."

"Yes, yes, oh, yes," she cried and cried until her hour was done.

"There you go, you can put your robe on. I need to get ready for the next client."

Marta replaced her robe and thanked him. "You are very good."

"So I've been told." He grinned.

She stepped outside and saw Consuela approach, quickly whispering instructions to her.

Consuela nodded and walked into the cabana.

Carlos noticed the exotic creature and immediately hardened. "Well, hello," he murmured. "Take your robe off and lie on the table." He held a towel in front of him after replacing the sheet and rose petals.

She removed her robe and gracefully mounted the table, sitting on the end, swinging her legs. "How do you want me?"

"Oh, hard and fast and slow and long," Carlos muttered, eyeing off the delicate long legs and high, perfect breasts.

Her eyes widened. "What?" She had never heard of

such a term, and coming from such a gorgeous man, she did not know what to think.

"Do you...ah..." He licked his lips. "Know what happens in here?" Standing in front of her all wet and slick, he desperately wanted the young thing sitting on the table.

Her eyes stayed wide. "Massages..." she managed. The man was gorgeous and making her heart pound. She'd never seen any man look like this, and definitely not her husband-to-be, or the boys back in her village. But he was different. He was exotic. Not white, not Greek, an exotic mixture of both.

His fingers travelled up her leg to her inner thigh. "I can do more than massage."

Those fingers made her feel things she had never felt before. Her stomach wrenched, her nipples hardened, and she felt wet between her legs. She swallowed and did as she was told.

Carlos's fingers slid into her bikini bottom and pulled them down as she lifted herself. He slid his shorts down, and she saw his erection moving toward her. It was something she had never seen before, a naked man, a penis, nor experienced in any way, shape, or form. Why would she have? She was just a young girl from a small Peruvian village. He lifted her up and onto him.

"Argh," she cried, having never been taken by a man before. Wrapping her arms around him, clinging to him as he gently slid back and forth, she cried out again. The pain from the first time was mixed with the pleasure he gave her.

His tongue invaded her mouth as his manhood invaded her insides. His fingers and hands explored her as they held her, and she exploded into a million pieces she didn't know was called an orgasm.

"Consuela, you dirty little whore," Marta yelled. "What will your husband-to-be say?"

Carlos spun around; still attached to the girl, to see the woman he'd just given a massage to and a big brute of a guy holding a gun on him. "What the…?"

"But, Marta, you told me to," Consuela cried as Gustoff levelled the gun. "Gustoff, what are you doing?"

Carlos dumped her on the bed and turned as the shot rang out. He dived for his clothes and ran like hell, hearing the words…

"Is she dead…?"

"…Yes."

*****

Connie heard the ruckus and what sounded like a gunshot. Sticking her head out of her private ground floor room, she saw Carlos speed up to her.

"Quick, I need to hide."

She ushered him into her room and locked the door while he dressed. "Was that a gunshot I heard?"

"Yep," Carlos panted. "Some crazy guy pointed a gun at me while I was um…" He shrugged. There was no time for politeness. "Fucking a client and shot at us. I ran, but I think he got her. I think she's dead. I gotta get outta here."

"Wait just a minute, you should go now. I'll get you

to the ferry."

"No, I have to go home." He pushed his hair back as he moved for the door. "I have to get my bags, my money, my passport. I need to go home."

"You need to leave the island," Connie said and came up with a plan. "You go and get your things then find me at the wharf. I'll get you to Athens and the airport. Go, go get your things."

With a nod, he sped off home, barging through the door ten minutes later. He collected his suitcase and bag, changed his clothes, strapped his money belt under his shirt and left a letter for his family, who luckily were out because he could not answer any questions right now. He legged it down to the wharf, careful not to be seen, and hid in the shadows looking for Connie. She turned up with two trunks and a large bag.

"I need the ferry to Athens. I'm going shopping tomorrow," she said.

"Of course." The purser rang up her ticket and helped her carry the trunks over to the waiting area near Carlos. It was in the shadows, and he managed to sneak over to her without being seen.

She spied him and quickly unlocked the trunks. They were empty. "Get in. You can hide until the airport."

Carlos frowned. "I have to hide in your trunk?"

"Do you want people to find you?" she fiercely whispered. "It was all over the hotel by the time I left. The cops have been called and are on their way to your house."

He frowned deeper. They'd find the letter.

"I saw the big brute of a guy and that girl. She was screaming bloody murder that you had tried to rape her and were raping her friend when they came upon you. They said you shot the girl."

"What!" Carlos exploded, but quickly quietened down, slinking back into the shadows. "*I did no such thing.* She was my client. I thought she was there for sex."

"Apparently she shouldn't have been there at all. She's set to marry some Greek bigwig, but had sneaked out just a week before the wedding while he was out of town."

"Look, I know nothing about that, but some thug tried to shoot me so I need to get out of here." He eyed the trunk. "Even if this is the only way."

They heard footsteps and saw Vivian Villiers approaching. "Darling, what have you gotten yourself into?" She held her arms open for him.

Carlos embraced her. "I have no idea, Viv, but I need to get the hell out of town."

"Well, isn't it a good thing I decided to come along. I know the perfect way to get you out," she said, eyeing their surroundings for anything suspicious.

"How?"

"Just get in the trunk, darling."

Carlos frowned again, but resigned his fate to an expensive Louis Vuitton trunk. He managed to fold his frame into the trunk and use his bag as a pillow.

"I'll put your case in the other trunk," Connie said and quickly packed it *and* Carlos up as the ferry approached.

Vivian went off to score herself a ticket, and within half an hour they were aboard the ferry to Athens where they arrived within the hour.

The ride was rough for Carlos; he'd never been sea sick but was feeling it now. And the pursers dumping him on the boat hadn't helped. Being dropped a few times made him want to vomit, but Viv and Connie had been able to open the trunk a crack on the way over to give him air until they were on the dock and he was being off-loaded again.

Ugh, this is worse than being shot at. What the hell was that all about? Who was that guy? Why was that woman I'd just massaged standing beside him? And what did it have to do with the girl I was inside of? Jesus, Jesus, Jesus, he silently cursed. *What the hell is going on?*

The trunk was lifted and dropped.

"Careful," Connie cried out. "That is a very expensive Louis Vuitton, and if you damage it, you pay for another one."

There were some more mumblings he couldn't hear and then they were moving. He checked his glow-in-the-dark watch. Ten after ten. He felt every bump and lump as they made their way to the airport, at least he hoped that's where they were going, and checked his watch again when they stopped. Ten-thirty.

The trunk was hefted down and carried up. Where he didn't know. They made a right turn, walked, made a left turn, and he was put down. The voices receded then there was another thud beside him, and more voices receded. He heard Connie and Viv come into the room and they opened the trunk.

"Bucket," was the first word out of his mouth and Viv managed to grab a champagne bucket just as he vomited.

"Ugh." She grimaced.

Carlos looked up. "You try getting around in a trunk and see if you can keep it all down." She gave him a towel to wipe his mouth. "Where are we?"

"On a private jet owned by a very good friend of mine." Viv sat on the bed and watched Carlos stumble out of the trunk. He hefted his bag out with him. "We don't need to show our passports, we can just go."

"You managed that?" Connie asked. "I was going to put him on a public plane."

Viv smiled mischievously. "Private is better, and the friend owed me a favour. No one knows we're on here. But I will have to let the pilot know. Let's take a seat." She went to tell the pilot, and he filed the flight plan. Ten minutes later they were winging their way to Hollywood.

"What am I going to do?" Carlos paced back and forth down the aisle. "I have no idea who those people were, what they wanted, or who they were after. Were they after me or the girl?"

"Nobody really knows," Viv told him. "All I heard was a bunch of screaming as I walked through the lobby. The girl was screaming that you had raped her and were attacking her friend. And her fiancé had tried to save them both."

"That's basically what I heard," Connie said.

"I've never raped anyone in my life," Carlos spat

angrily. With the week he'd had he was pissed off big time. He ran a hand through his hair. "What am I gonna do?" Slumping into his seat, he repeated, "What am I gonna do?"

Viv and Connie sat side by side, dressed to the nines in their finery, having left half of their belongings on the island. But hotel staff would send them later. They looked at each other, a plan formulating in their minds.

"Well, darling, it looks like you'll have to go on the run. Change your name, live in another country."

"Away from my parents, my brothers, my job?" He didn't like saying it, let alone thinking it.

"I don't think you'll have that anymore, darling," Connie said. "You're wanted for rape and murder. You wouldn't keep your job."

Carlos sighed. "My life has just gone to shit."

"Not necessarily. Have you thought about pursuing that career I talked to you about?" Viv asked.

His brain was so fogged he didn't comprehend what she was saying. "What career?"

The women shared a glance. "Your porn star career."

Carlos tilted his head. "You expect me to take on a public career knowing full well someone's just tried to kill me and has accused me of rape? I'm an escapee!" he reminded them. "They get one look at me in a movie and they'll know exactly where I am and come and get me."

"Not necessarily," Connie said. "We change your name, maybe your hair…"

He frowned. "How much am I supposed to change

in order to stay out of the fuzz's way? How long am I supposed to keep running?"

"Well," Viv replied. "Maybe you don't have to." She exchanged another glance with Connie. "A certain producer we know happens to be good friends with certain people in certain places. If you make money for him, he will make things disappear."

"Things?"

"Problems."

"Like murder and rape charges?" Carlos raised a brow. "He can't be that good."

"Oh, he's very good," Connie said.

"You'd be amazed at what he can do," Viv added.

Carlos shook his head. "I don't think anyone can save me. Hell, I don't even know what the hell is going on." He was tired. All of his energy had been sucked out of him in the last ten hours, and now he was spent.

"Why don't you go and lie down in one of the bedrooms," Viv said. "We could all do with a rest."

"Mmm." His eyes were already half closed. "Okay." He slowly made his way back to the bedroom where Connie's trunks were, grabbed a pillow, and was out like a light.

They landed in L.A. fifteen hours later and woke him up. "Time to leave darling," Connie said.

He yawned. "Where are we?"

"We're in L.A.," Viv said, coming into the room. "I've made some calls, and our passports will be checked on board, but we should be free to go after that."

"Our passports? But they'll know where I'm from."

Carlos felt panic start to rise, but squelched it down.

"That's what one of my calls was about," Viv said, collecting her things. "The person doing the checking is a big fan of mine and will see to it personally we are let through. And as far as I know, nothing has hit the newspapers over here yet, so it's probably been contained on Mykonos."

Carlos thought about his family. *What the hell must they be thinking? Had they read the letter? Or had the cops gotten to them?*

"Don't worry; we'll lie low at my place for a few days while we get some things sorted out. Then we'll help you start your future," Connie said.

"Will it be a future where I'm not arrested and charged with murder and rape?" Carlos asked.

The women shrugged. "Who knows?"

"Great. So you can't even guarantee it."

"Hello, Miss Vivian, it is Marco," a voice called out.

They stopped.

How much had he heard?

Vivian left the room to greet him. "Of course, Marco, how are you darling?"

"Oh, very good, Miss Vivian, I am here to look at your passports."

"Of course. Here's mine, the others are just getting theirs."

Connie and Carlos retrieved theirs and walked into the aisle.

"Ah, oh, my God." Marco's eyes lingered upon Carlos, and Carlos panicked. "You are gorgeous," Marco went on, so clearly gay. "And what is *your* name?" He held out his hand.

"Carlos," he said simply and handed over his papers.

Next, Marco checked Connie's and handed them back. "And you are here in L.A. for?"

"Work," Viv said. "Boring!"

"Play," Connie said smugly.

Carlos said nothing.

"Well, everything is in order," Marco said, handing back passports. "Enjoy your stay ladies." He eyed the gorgeous Adonis before him. "Carlos," he purred and turned on his heel.

Once he was gone, Viv laughed. "You certainly got off to a good gay start. One fan down, five million to go."

"Yes, and speaking of going, is the limo ready?" Connie asked, peering through a window.

"Ready and waiting," Viv said.

"Good, let's go."

They carried out bags and trunks and settled into the back of the limo. The ride took half an hour to wind their way through Laurel Canyon and pull up at the high metal gates which buzzed open. The chauffeur drove them up to the front door.

Climbing out, Carlos saw a huge one level home spreading left and right with thick greenery, bushes and trees, large windows, and a high brick wall.

Connie showed Carlos to a bedroom with a view of the pool out back. "This is for you, darling. The whole wing is yours. I'm at the other end."

Carlos cocked a brow. "You mean you don't want me staying with you?"

Connie's wicked laugh echoed around the room. "I

wish. But you're not on the job while you're here, you're my guest, so I will leave you alone. Come outside when you've freshened up."

Carlos opened his suitcase and pulled out his clothes. T-shirts, jeans, basic necessities and nothing fancy. In his bag was a small variety of clothes and personal effects. They had been packed in there for over a year now. His getaway plan for when he left Mykonos. Except that would have been on his twenty-fifth birthday with a one-way ticket to somewhere. Now he was in Hollywood at twenty-four with a one-way ticket and the prospect of never seeing his family again. He put his things in the huge walk-in closet and took a shower in the large tiled bathroom. Dressed in the clothes he'd left out, he met Connie, who'd also changed, and Viv by the pool.

Huge serving platters of food were on the table and jugs filled with juice, coffee and water sat next to them.

"Help yourself, darling, you must be famished." Connie shoved a forkful of omelette into her mouth.

He wasn't, but the smell made his stomach grumble, and he piled a plate high with food.

Viv got off the phone as he put the first spoonful into his mouth. "I just spoke to Harry about your problem. At first, he didn't want to help sight unseen, but Connie and I convinced him you're worth it, so he's helping you. He's getting his private investigators to Mykonos today to find out what's going on and to track down those two people. We're going to find out who they are and what they're up to."

Carlos swallowed and took a gulp of juice. "Is it

wise to tell people?"

"Harry runs a porn studio; privacy is his middle name. If the secrets about his actors got out he'd be in deep financial trouble, so keeping secrets and personal issues out of the press is his speciality."

"So, if I work for Harry, he'll cover up my past?"

"As much as he can," Viv said. "Well, he covered up *my* porn movies."

Carlos looked up in surprise. "*You? You* were in pornos?"

"When I was a wee lass," Viv said, blushing in embarrassment. "I hated the fact I'd done them and regretted it badly, but I needed the money and didn't do any more. Harry covered them up."

"Wait, *you* did porn movies, and hate that you did, but you want to push *me* into doing them instead?" Carlos was confused by the weird contradiction.

Viv shrugged. "It wasn't for me. But it is for you and I think with your talent…" She squeezed his hand. "You'll go a long way and be a big, big star. Big…huge!" She held her hands about two feet apart.

"I'm not that big." Despite his love of sex, it was still embarrassing for him to hear women talk like that.

"It's true," Viv replied. "And Harry wants to meet you tomorrow."

"That soon?"

"That soon."

He nodded. "Okay. Is it safe for me to get around? How will I get there and where am I going?"

"For a start, Connie and I will be taking you in her limo, so you don't need to worry about getting there or being seen. And second, we'll be going to their house so it will be a private setting."

"And what will I need to do? Do I need to perform?" He raised a brow jauntily. "With one of you?"

Connie tittered.

"Oh, you've already performed." Viv blushed. "Probably not, no, you will need to show him your goods, so wear something you can slip out of easily."

"So, like every other day of my life then," Carlos joked despite the seriousness of the situation.

"Pretty much," Connie said.

"And then what?"

"Then you have a career as an actor," Viv replied. "You'll be famous."

He pulled a face. "Great."

"You just relax for the rest of today and catch up on your beauty sleep. You still look tired. I'll be back tomorrow," Viv said, getting up.

Carlos rose and hugged her. "Thank you, for everything." They kissed.

"Anything for you, darling." She wiped his mouth free from her lipstick. "See you tomorrow. Connie." She waved and disappeared into the house.

Carlos spent the afternoon relaxing by the pool, catching up on the news, and reading the magazines Connie had by the bucket load around the house. He caught up on local celebrities, his favourite bands, and who was supposedly doing whom in Hollywood circles. He watched programs he'd never seen before on TV and wondered in amazement at all the things he'd missed out on living in Mykonos.

He followed up a delicious late dinner with a swim in the pool, and floating on his back, he looked up into the night sky at the millions of stars and thought how they looked so different when viewed from the other side of the globe. He wondered about his family, how they were coping and if they were in trouble. He hoped not, but then considering what had happened he couldn't be sure. After taking one last swim, he headed inside for bed.

*****

In the morning, Viv arrived with some news. "Harry's investigators are in Mykonos and have contacted your family. They're okay and not in any trouble."

Carlos sighed and leant back in his seat, breakfast forgotten. "That's good."

Viv looked at her watch. "We'd better get going. Harry and Harriet are dying to meet you."

They quickly finished breakfast and made their way to the limo for the ride to Harry DeVille's private residence. The drive took them twenty minutes, and they entered a gated driveway with a long winding drive that wound its way up to an impressively sprawling two-storey house.

"Wow." Carlos stared as he looked up at the place.

"The house that porn built," Viv told him.

"How many has he done?" Carlos asked, turning around to gaze at the expansive lawns and gardens.

"One thousand, two hundred and forty-three," Connie said. "But who's counting?"

"And how many built this house?"

"One hundred and two," Viv said.

They walked up the huge stone steps and were greeted by the butler. "Mr and Mrs DeVille will see you in the office," he said.

"Thank you, Deveers," Viv said warmly and led the way down the hall on their right into a maze of rooms full of bedroom, office, and street scenes with cameras, lighting, and screens. They walked into the office and came face to face with Harry and Harriet who were ready and waiting for them.

"So, what do we have here?" Harry DeVille said, getting up from behind his desk and walking over to stand in front of them. "Let's see the goods."

Carlos pulled his t-shirt over his head and stepped out of his pants.

Harry DeVille's eyes lit up at the golden tanned Adonis with the ten inch cock before him. "My, you are perfect."

Harriet licked her lips and fingered the pearls around her neck. "I want to try him out."

Harry arched a brow. "Me first."

August 1977

Carlos was on the set of his very first porn movie, sitting in a director's chair with his name on the back, reading his script and running through his lines. He glanced around the room, a room in Harry DeVille's home, set up like a studio with lights and cameras and made to look like a cabana.

Talk about art imitating life.

Harry had taken one look at Carlos that fateful day two months ago and knew he was everything he'd heard about from Harriet, who'd heard about it from Connie and Viv. The half Greek Adonis was everything he'd wanted, and Harry knew exactly how to make him a star. He'd use the same concept of what Carlos's life had been. Resorts, cabanas, and private massages.

He'd had his writers get a script together, hired his best actress, and set about turning Carlos Stephanopoulos into Carlo Stefan, the biggest and brightest porn star in his stable.

Of course, the name change was important, even though it didn't take a genius to figure it out. But at least the cops weren't looking for him. No, Harry's PIs had turned up some very interesting information about the crime committed, the people behind it, and how it had affected all involved. He assured Carlos all was okay, and so was he.

"Well, my boy." Harry slapped Carlos on the back. "How are you today?" He sat in the chair beside him.

Carlos smiled. He hadn't minded the name change or the new hair style, but reliving his life on the island was straight out weird. "Good, Harry," he said. "But this is just…" He waved the script in the air. "Reliving my life. It's nothing different, nothing new."

"No, no, Carlos; it's not. But one look at you after the stories I'd heard and I knew that women worldwide would want you to massage them…" he winked, "in every way. It's perfect for you. With your looks, look at you." Harry eyed him up and down. Carlos had kept the tan up while in L.A. and worked out to stay in shape. "Women are going to die over you."

Carlos's smile was still in place. "I hope you're right. I'd hate to be a failure and let you down. Especially after everything you've done."

"The only way you've let me down is by not letting me try out the goods."

"I don't swing that way, Harry."

"I know, and I respect that. Doesn't mean I can't be unhappy about it. How are you holding up with everything else going on?"

Carlos nodded. "Good. I talked to my family yesterday. Both of my brothers have left the island, but my parents are still there. They're grateful the whole thing has died down and all but disappeared."

"Yeah." Harry sucked on his cigar. "Even I'm surprised about that one. Some bigwig from Athens is involved somehow and shut it down pretty quick. Didn't want the publicity apparently."

"Do we know who the bigwig is?" Carlos ran a hand through his now short-ish hair that was the latest style for men.

"That was all kept hush-hush." Harry blew smoke rings. "I'm thinking he paid off the Greek Feds to keep it quiet."

"Am I still wanted for murder and rape?"

"Not that we could see. The charges seem to have disappeared."

"Just like my brothers." Carlos sighed.

"Your parents holding up with all the kids out of the nest?"

Carlos smiled. "Barely. All of Mama's babies have fled the nest within months of each other. Papa… well…he's pissed off about his son's legal issues and that we won't be working in the meat shop this winter."

"Do meat shops do good business in winter?"

Carlos laughed. "With the three of us working there, yeah. Everyone buys from us in the winter, and all the other stores complain they get no customers. *'Your sons are putting us out of business,'* they complain. *'Good,'* Papa says, *'then I'll be the only meat shop on the island'.*"

"Meat shop, huh." An idea formed in Harry's mind. "Meat...shop..."

"Yeah." Carlos saw the faraway look on Harry's face. "What are you thinking?"

"A great idea, kid. A big money-maker involving meat." Harry slapped him on the back and stood up. "And you're the meat." He walked away laughing.

"Okay, we're ready to go," the director yelled. "Carlo, Neesa, take your places. The lighting's ready, camera's ready. Harry!"

Everyone took their positions.

Carlos was standing in the cabana in his white tank and shorts. The curtains billowed softly, fake candles were lit. The massage table was covered in a white sheet and rose petals. He shivered, remembering the last time he'd been in a place like that.

"Ready on set...three...two...one...action..."

Carlos was tidying the towels when an exotic beauty walked in. Creamy chocolate skin, long limbs, short hair, and a mouth as big as it needed to be to take a man into it.

"Well, hello," Carlos greeted. "Lie face down on the table and we'll get started.

"Oh, no, darling." She slid her one-piece straps off her shoulders, down her body, and stepped out of it, much to Carlos's satisfaction. "I prefer face up." She gracefully sat on the bed, swung her long, lithe legs up and lay down. She arched her back slightly to push her large breasts up, and bent her legs, spreading them for all to see. "Come, darling. Massage me from the inside out."

Carlos took his time, even though his cock wanted to get things going now. He massaged her legs up to her inner thighs.

"Ugh, oh," she groaned, arching. "Come, darling, come."

Carlos slipped off his clothes and mounted the table between her legs. Pushing them down, he manoeuvred himself so his knees were outside of hers, her legs now shut.

She arched higher. "Ugh, take me, darling, take me."

His hands did their magic across her abdomen and up over her breasts.

"Ugh, oh, God." She clenched the sheets. "Oh, God, you're good."

A wicked smile spread across Carlos's face, and he shifted position so he was sitting farther up. His penis lay between her breasts as he gently squeezed them together, massaging all three at once.

Her nipples were harder and larger than he'd ever seen, and so was he. He forgot there was a camera crew watching and felt as if he was back home working. Working the exotic beauties he'd had every lunchtime, every night-time. His hands moved up to her shoulders and throat, massaging the muscles to relieve the stiffness.

"Oh, God, come," she rasped. "I'm coming, come, come."

Carlos shifted again. In one motion he knelt, tucked her arms under his legs and sat on her breasts. He lifted her head and led her mouth to his cock that was so ready to be sucked. "Come," he commanded. "Come."

She sucked greedily as he controlled her head, thrusting it back and forth over his shaft. He groaned and his head flung back. "Suck, suck." Faster and faster he thrust her head and she clung to the table, groaning and moaning. And before she knew it she flung her legs up around his shoulders trying to lock her ankles in place. He flung them away, but she pulled her knees up and grabbed his arms, letting the world see it all. She didn't care. He didn't care. They showed the world that they came together.

It was over, and they stopped in the same positions, panting, sweating.

He released her head. She released him. And they relaxed until he slid down her body and off the table. He dressed and offered her a towel.

She lay there. "That was the best massage I've ever had."

"Glad to have pleased you," he said and walked out of the cabana.

"And…cut," the director yelled…finally…

Carlos walked from behind the cabana. "How was I?"

Everyone stared at him, even Neesa, in dead silence, and when he frowned, one by one they started applauding, starting with Harry. He even got a standing ovation.

Carlos reddened, his cheeks burning his face. He'd only ever been applauded by some of the women he'd serviced, not by a room full of men.

Harry came over to him with Harriet not far behind. "My boy." He slapped him on the back. "You've just made us a million dollars."

"Really?" Carlos's eyes widened. "You'll sell that much?"

"Maybe more." Harry walked him over to his chair.

"Oh, if only you'd do that to me, Carlos," Harriet said with Neesa behind her. "I would love for you to do that to me."

"I'd love for you to do that to me *again*," Neesa said. "I don't know how you did it, honey, but you have learned things and know things that I've never seen any man know. There's definitely something about you." She fondled his hair as she stood by his side. "Definitely something about you."

"It's the half Greek thing," Harry said matter-of-factly. "Look at him. Golden body, muscles up to here…" Harry indicated with a hand to his face. "Big blue eyes, golden hair. He's the Golden God."

"I like the sound of that." Harriet fluttered in front of him, pawing at his knee.

Harry nodded. "Yeah, yeah, so do I. From now on you're Carlo Stefan, the Golden God. And we'll do more than just Cabana movies. I've got a few ideas forming. *God-like* ideas."

Harriet gasped. "Oh, I know. Do supernatural movies. He's the God of Greece and he comes down to be serviced by all the different women every night." She rubbed his leg, her hand moving higher which he politely moved away with a gentle squeeze.

"You got it, Harriet. Reading my mind again. David," Harry bellowed, and a young guy in his twenties with short brown hair and glasses came running over with a clipboard. "Take down this idea."

Harry led him away as he belted out his thoughts and David tried keeping up with them.

"Is that it for today?" Carlos asked.

"We may need to do another take." Neesa tickled his ear. "Just in case they didn't get it all the first time."

Carlos grinned. "Are you up for it again?"

"Well, if you do *that* again, I'm up for anything."

His grin got bigger. "So am I."

As it turned out, they only needed to do a few checks for lights and sound and that was it, much to Neesa's disappointment.

Carlos's first day on the set was done.

*****

Viv, Connie, and Carlos rocked up to *Troubadour*, one of L.A.'s biggest clubs, that night for a celebration. The whole cast and crew were partying, thanks to Harry, for a job well done and a future to look forward to.

Carlos felt out of his league. Every which way he turned there were celebrities, musicians, and actors. Robert Redford, Michael Jackson, Johnny Carson.

Viv led them to the corner of the club and picked up three glasses of champagne, handing one each to Connie and Carlos.

"Carlos, my boy," Harry yelled out from his prime position in the centre of the space where he was surrounded by beautiful women and gorgeous men, plus staff and crew. "Welcome to the world of sex. Cheers."

"Cheers."

Champagne, wine, beer, all flowed freely. Cocaine,

acid and painkillers were snorted, popped or injected even more freely, and Carlos found himself veering away to the centre of the room with its dance floor, loud thumping music, and hypnotic beats. He found himself taken away, just as his nights on Mykonos. He danced up a storm with women wanting to dance with him and men wanting to kill him…except for the guys who wanted to fuck him as badly as the women.

Carlos watched the room and the people in it. His white suit and black shirt brought out the tanned skin and golden locks. His dance moves brought everyone to him, and he found himself dancing with a girl who looked too innocent to be at a club like that.

She stood wide-eyed as he gyrated and thrust at her, not moving, clutching her purse to her chest. The rose-coloured dress with its skinny straps brought rosiness to her cheeks, and her long curly hair was swept back with rose barrettes.

Carlos finally noticed how spooked she looked and stopped dancing. "Are you okay?" He leant in, his hand on her elbow.

"What?" She couldn't hear him.

He waved a hand toward the exit and guided her through the crowd until they made their way outside to the relative peace and quiet. "Whew, that was noisy," Carlos said, leading the girl a few feet away from the crowd waiting to get in. "Now." He turned to face her. "Are you okay?"

"Uh." She gazed up at the gorgeous man she'd allowed to lead her away from her friends. "Why wouldn't I be okay?"

"Because you looked scared and out of place." Carlos took in her features. Big brown eyes, button nose, rose-red lips. She was slim, pretty, and he was stirring.

"I'm…fine…" she said slowly, not sure she should even be standing on the street with a man that looked like a god, let alone outside of the club she'd tried for a whole year to get into.

"Well, you didn't look it." He saw her shivering, took off his blazer, and laid it around her shoulders.

"Oh." She looked everywhere but at him. "Thank you."

"I'm Carlos. What's your name?" He was close enough to smell her scent.

She smelt his and breathed it in. "Rosalee."

Their eyes connected.

Their lips connected.

Their tongues connected.

And before anyone knew it he had her against the wall in the alley next to the club.

"Ah, oh, oh." She arched against the wall, head back, knickers down, leg hooked over his arm and around his waist. He filled her, and she felt every glorious inch of him.

Fear, surprise, passion, desire, all finally ripped through her as he picked her up and she wrapped her other leg around him. "Oh, God," she screamed as he buried himself in her.

Carlos grunted. It was good to have plain old sex again. Picking up some woman and having his way. It wasn't paid for, wasn't booked in, and wasn't a performance. It was pure pleasurable sex, and he hadn't gotten that since Mykonos. Not even Connie or Viv had wanted his services.

He came to a screaming halt and slowly let her slip back to the ground. Releasing himself, he tucked it away as she dazedly pulled up her knickers and smoothed down her dress. "What do you say we go back to my place?" He'd gotten a small apartment at the beach a month ago because he didn't want to live off Connie anymore, and with the money he'd saved from six years of resort work he'd had enough for a hefty down payment.

Rosalee stood staring at him. "Who are you?"

He frowned. "Uh, Carlos."

She blushed. "I know. I meant who *are* you? Are you a celebrity, actor?"

"Yeah…actor."

She turned the same pretty colour as her dress. "Have I seen you in anything?"

"Not yet. I just shot it today."

"Oh, when will it be out?"

"Next month."

"And you have your own place?"

"Yep, wanna go?"

"Yes."

He took her hand and they hailed the limo that had brought him there. After giving the address to the driver, he sat back and they sipped champagne from the mini bar.

"So, it's your first movie?" she asked quietly.

"Yep."

"Will you be doing anymore?"

"I have a whole list of them ready to go."

The alcohol added to the headiness of post sex and they were already locking lips by the time they stumbled into his bedroom and onto his massive animal print covered bed.

"I don't normally do this," she whispered as he slid her underwear down and her dress up before lying naked under his expert hands.

"Do what?" He quickly undressed and lay beside her, pulling a satin sheet over them.

"Have sex with a man I don't know in a cheap alley and then go home with him to fall into bed." She sighed at the touch of his hand.

"Well, there's a first time for everything." His lips followed his fingers and explored her body. She sighed at every touch, every kiss, and he felt like a normal twenty-four-year-old again. He'd never fallen in love before.

Love!

Where the hell did that come from?

But the feelings he was having lying next to her were vastly different to what he felt while he was fucking every other woman. No, *she* was vastly different. She wasn't out for sex, it had just happened. They had met, been attracted, and it had just happened. Now, he was feeling good about it. And it wasn't bought and paid for.

"Oh, Carlos," she murmured as his fingers found their way between her legs, she arched, instinctively spreading her legs to allow him access. And he obliged, sliding into her as though he had all the time in the world.

Sex was slow, rhythmic, and they rested in between each session, drinking champagne, eating various fruits and berries he kept in the fridge. They talked, they kissed, they made love. They were so enamoured with each other they didn't notice the shadow on the balcony.

The man peered through the half-open curtain. The room was mostly dark except for a few candles, but he could make out Carlos Stephanopoulos and the young brunette he was bedding.

Continuously.

"Doesn't he ever stop," muttered the man who'd managed to climb over the first floor balcony to Carlos's second floor apartment. Feeling highly inadequate, he pulled his straining cock out and relieved himself on the pot plant. He'd seen the little thing she was and had found himself hard at the way her lithe young body moved. Now he was letting his own seed go before making his way back down to the ground. "Ugh," he grunted, getting to his feet. He hurried back down the street to his car, drove to the nearest phone booth, and rang his boss. "Yeah, I found him. I know where he lives. Yeah, with a woman. Young, pretty. Can't keep it in his pants. Yeah, keep following, yeah, okay. Take them both out. Got it."

September 1977

Carlos stepped out of the limousine to flashbulbs and screaming, standing on the red carpet, savouring the attention, wearing a blue suit and white shirt.

Harry and Harriet stepped out behind him and stood either side. "Well, you've made it, my boy."

"How could I have made it when the movie hasn't even been seen yet?" Carlos waved at fans as they made their way up the carpet.

"Because the trailer that's been playing has everyone so damn hot. So do all of the photos we've released."

Carlos blew kisses to fans as they went inside *The Pussycat Theatre* on Santa Monica Boulevard. The theatre was the place to be to debut all porno movies, and tonight was Carlos's night. It had been a month since he'd filmed it, and he'd made three more since. Now, Harry was setting him up with other ideas.

He shook hands with some of the industry's leaders, and kissed Connie on the cheek before they took their seats inside. Half an hour later they emerged to explosive clapping and whistling. The movie had gone down well, and they were heading back to Harry's for the after-party.

"So, what next?" Carlos asked from his seat in the back of the limo.

"We release it from tonight and make that million I told you about," Harry said.

"I meant with my career. The movies. What next?"

"Well, we've got that meat shop movie up next, based on your days working there, so that's in pre-production right now. Just have to get the scripts in a couple of days." Harry lit his cigar and puffed.

"Great, so one a week then?"

"One a week."

"Do I get a pay rise?"

"Oh, you definitely get a rise." Harry patted his crotch.

"Harry," Carlos admonished. "Not what I meant."

Harry guffawed. "I know. We'll see how well these Cabana movies go and then talk business."

"And I've been thinking," Carlos said as they rolled up to the house. "I want to be a part of it. A bigger part. I want more control over the way I'm portrayed. I may have made a living from being the resident masseur in the cabana, but I want to be more than that. I want to dictate my future. After all…" He got out of the limo. "My career will be over by the time I'm thirty."

"Not necessarily, my boy." Harry led the way into his house. "If you continue looking that good, you could keep going until your forty or older."

They stepped into the expansive and obscenely decorated living and entertainment room and were enveloped in a sea of staff, crew, celebrities, other porn actors, movie actors, and all manner of people who came to one of Harry DeVille's personal parties.

A glass of champagne was shoved into Carlos's hand, and a stirringly gorgeous brunette led him to two crowded sofas full of hot randy women.

"Carlos," they cooed. "Come join us."

"Or just come," a wickedly delightful African American with cropped hair and large red lips said. She opened her mouth wide. "Oh, yes, do come."

Heat raced over Carlos's face, and he was sure he was beet red. Of course, he was used to horny women hitting on him, but here in Hollywood, it was so blatant. "How about we leave that for another day." He was pulled down onto the couch full of women, finding himself lying across their laps and being fondled. "Hey, ladies." He turned on his back, and the black woman with the big mouth unzipped his pants, pulled out his cock, and started sucking it.

"Whoa, hey, not now. Leave it out. Hey." He was covered in a sea of women as they gathered around to feed on the cock of Adonis.

"Hey." His voice became deep and guttural as they all took him. "Hello, ladies." He grabbed the head of the blonde whose lap he rested his head on and pulled her lips to his. He was sucked and tongued by the women, and at some stage thought he saw a man in the pool, which brought him to his senses. "Whoa, okay, that's enough." He rolled off the women, jumped up, and stumbled over them as he made his way outside while trying to put it back in and zip himself up.

"Oh, come back, Carlos. We want more."

He ran out into the backyard and around the penis-shaped pool to the other side, trying to get some space, and time, to recuperate. He felt used, not that he hadn't enjoyed it, but it wasn't work, and he wasn't getting paid. It was just a bunch of horny women hungrily attacking a horny man. He pushed his hair back. "Jesus!"

"Hello, Carlos."

Spinning around, he came face to face with the Hollywood starlet who'd given him head back in Mykonos. He couldn't think of her name then, and couldn't think of it now. "Hey, you came to my cabana on Mykonos."

"That's right." Her blonde hair was piled on her head with loose curls hanging around her face. She wore a tight, short purple dress with slashes down to her crotch. The back was the same. Purple stilettoes, fiery red lipstick, and some gold jewellery finished off the outfit. She walked seductively up to him. Face to face they stood, while her fingers did their job and her tongue occupied his.

He pushed her away. "I'm off the clock."

"I'll pay." She pulled a wad of hundreds from her gold clutch. "Just like last time…" Casting a glance back at the house she said, "Unlike all of those women that took advantage of you in there."

"How much?" He eyed the money.

"One thousand for a quick fuck wasn't it?" Her lips nuzzled his.

He breathed. "All right."

She pushed him backwards, and they found themselves at the back of the pool house, with her plastered against the wall, her dress around her waist, and her legs around his as he ploughed into her.

"Suck it, suck my tit," she demanded as she was smashed into the wall. She felt the roughness and knew her back would be marked.

His mouth closed around the rubbery nipple and sucked it into a hard lump.

"Harder, suck harder," she cried, gripping his jacket while trying not to break a nail. "Fuck me, fuck me, oh, oh, oh…"

Carlos finished with a final thrust and waited to catch his breath before letting her slide to her feet. He put it away, straightened his clothes, and caught his breath, watching as she put her dress back in place.

"Oh, God," she groaned. "I love it hard and fast. Here." Holding out her hand with the money she snatched it away when he went to take it. She leant against him, pulled his pant waist out and shoved the money down his shorts. "It deserves it," she purred and left him to go back to the party.

He pocketed the cash and waited until she was in the house before carefully making his way to a bench in the garden. Sure it was all about free love, but did he need Harry to know he made some on the side?

Pushing his hair back, he breathed deeply, gazing up into the sky, wondering about his parents. He phoned once a month to be safe, and while they were okay, they hated their sons not being there. And his brothers? Where the hell were they? Pedro was only twenty, Tomas twenty-two. He hoped they weren't getting themselves into anything like he'd done and that they were safe.

"Carlos, my boy, what are you doing out here?" Harry plodded over and sat beside him. At sixty-six he was feeling old, and his body was showing it. His hair was grey and thinning, his skin was over-tanned and sagging. He was no longer the great actor-producer of his time. Well, not in the old way, but he was in the porn way, and he was making a killing.

"Taking a break." Carlos continued staring up at the sky.

"You're one of those now."

"One of what?"

"A star!"

Carlos grinned. "Ya think?"

"I know," Harry said matter-of-factly. "All those women get to ya did they?"

Carlos laughed. "In more ways than one."

"So I saw."

Silence.

"Harry?"

"Mmm?"

"What I said before…I was serious."

"About what?"

"Taking control of my future."

"So, what do you want to do?"

"I want final say on the scripts. There's not much

to them, but I want them to be realistic and authentic. To me anyway."

"Okay kid, you can get a look at the scripts."

"I want final say."

"We'll see when they come in."

October 1977

A few days later they were reading the scripts for the meat shop scenario.

"This is awful." Carlos threw his script down on the table. "It's not even what would happen in a real meat shop."

Harry agreed that it wasn't the best. "But it's not a real meat shop. So what do you want to do?"

"Give me a couple of hours to come up with something and I'll show you." Carlos went back to his apartment, drew on previous experience, and wrote a script. He threw it down in front of Harry two and a half hours later. "*This* is real."

Harry read through it, nodding, making faces, making small sounds. He put down the papers. "This is much better than the tripe David presented me with."

"That's because he looks as if he hasn't had any experience doing those things."

"He hasn't," Harry bellowed. "And maybe that's the problem." He got up and paced around his desk. "Carlos, my boy. If you can write that, then lend your hands to a few other ideas and we'll see how things go. Do you think you can give me four more of those?" He waved at the script on his desk.

"Already in the works, Harry." Carlos grinned. "The ideas came to me and I made notes. I'll write them up tonight."

"Good, good." Harry clamped a hand on Carlos's shoulder. "You'll be getting credits for them; hence you'll make more money. Is that a good start to you having more control over your career?"

"It's a start," Carlos agreed.

*****

Two days later they were on the set at Harry's house, and one of the rooms had been set up like a meat shop. Carlos had a hand in the layout, explaining that since he was used to his father's store, it would be better and make him feel more comfortable if it was a layout he knew.

The cabinets were in place, filled with fake meat, the lighting was set just so, and Carlos and an exotic-looking woman called Mariska got into their outfits. He was to play the butcher in his white shirt, unbuttoned down to the navel, and white pants that had a spring lock on the front so he could rip them open in an instant. His butcher apron completed the look.

Mariska, herself of Greek lineage, with her long

dark glossy black hair that curled down to her waist, big black innocent eyes, and a wide lipped mouth, wore a simple floral dress that flared gently around her knees. She would be the innocent young maiden out to buy some meat, and he was the man to give it to her.

They took their places on set and waited for the director to yell *action.*

Mariska walked through the door followed by a gentle sea breeze which not only ruffled her hair but Carlos's as well.

He did a casual head flick in slow motion and set his blue eyes upon the young girl before him. "Hello, lovely young lady, what can I get for you?" He flexed his chest under the lights so the camera could pick up his golden chest hair.

"Oh," Mariska murmured. "I just came in for some… meat…"

"Then let me show you our selection." He pointed out the different cuts from various animals and waited at the counter while she stood making up her mind.

"I just don't know," she finally said through her big lips and innocent eyes. "Do you have any…sausage…?"

"Sausage! I'll show you sausage!" Carlos ripped his apron off and his pants undone to reveal his big Greek sausage at full attention. "It's ripe and hard and just waiting to put itself in your mouth." He lifted up the counter, stepped toward her, grabbed her waist and slammed her against the curved meat cabinet.

Tearing open her dress, he thrust that Greek sausage into her over and over while her arms flailed above her head.

"Oh, oh, I just came in for some meat." She hitched her legs up, and the camera zoomed in on her bouncing breasts, so big and full and juicy.

"Oh, oh, I love sausage," she groaned as Carlos kept going and going and going. "Oh, God, oh, God, you're so, oh, God, I can't take it anymore, oh, God, oh, God, help me. Oh, God, I'm going to explode, oh!" She convulsed on the orgasm, the likes she'd never felt. "Oh, God," she screamed and slammed her head against the cabinet. "Oh, God." She arched, she bent, she breathed.

And Carlos was done.

He held her while her legs slid down to the floor and leant into her, his hands on her breasts, kneading their voluptuousness. "And that is how you have sausage," he breathed into her neck.

"Oh, God," she groaned. "I love sausage. Give me more."

He slid out of her and helped her stand. "Not now, my little sausage lover. I have other customers to worry about." And with that, he put his sausage away, donned his apron and wrapped up a packet of sausages for her. "Your sausages." He presented her with the parcel.

She quickly did her dress up and took the package. "Thank you, I'll be back tomorrow."

"Yes," Carlos breathed. "*Come…*tomorrow."

She walked out the door, and Carlos went back to cutting meat.

"And…cut, print!" the director yelled. "Good job people. We've got a winner there."

Carlos walked off the stage and collapsed into his seat next to Mariska's. "Are you okay? You seemed to hit your head pretty hard."

She rubbed the back of her head. "I'm okay. It's not the first time I've hit something on a set. But that was the first time I've had an explosive orgasm like that. You're quite the master." Her gaze lowered to his crotch. "You definitely know that sausage can please a woman."

He grinned and leant on the chair arm toward her. "Years of practice and being told what to do by women."

"Well…" She sighed and gazed into his gorgeous eyes. "You definitely have been taught well and taken notice."

"All in here." He tapped his temple. "Catalogued and in order."

"Do you ever just *make love* to a woman?" Mariska asked, sipping an iced tea that the actors' assistant had brought her. "I haven't been able to have boyfriends because they all get the weirds about me having sex for a living. So I end up single."

Carlos thought back to Viv and Rosalee. "I used to. In Mykonos, I'd see different girls during lunchtime. Since then there've only been two ladies I've been with, but that reminds me to call one. I'll see you later." He ran off to change and then called Rosalee. He hadn't seen her in over a week and now felt like having a nice dinner and dancing. He called her home number. "Hey Rosalee, how about dinner and some dancing. I know a great place…Rosalee…"

"Uh-um," she stuttered. "Why don't you come over now? I…I…need you now."

"Um, yeah, sure. I'll see you soon." He raced out the door and drove to her place, wondering why she sounded so strange. *Out of it is more like it,* he thought. *But I didn't think she did drugs.* He parked outside of her small house, bounced up the stairs and knocked on the door. It creaked open. "Rosalee?" His hand pushed it further. "Rosalee?" Stepping inside, he closed it behind him. "Rosalee?" Walking past the small kitchen into the small lounge room he looked through the open door to the bedroom. She was lying naked, spread-eagled on her bed.

"Carlos," she lazily called. "I'm waiting." A giggle escaped from her lips. "Fuck me." She bent her legs and motioned him inside her. "Fuck me."

He stepped into the room and frowned. "Rosalee? Are you okay?" He'd never seen her in that state and wondered what she was on.

"Fuck me," she screamed at him, her womanhood on full display between spread legs. "Fuck me, Carlos, fuck me."

"Rosalee, I…"

She got to her knees and grabbed him, pulling him down on the bed, yanking his penis from his pants and sitting on it.

"Rosalee, I—"

"Fuck me, Carlos, woohoo." She waved her arms around. "Ride 'em cowboy." Her breasts bounced up and down, and her hair fell in curly waves. "Fuck me, fuck me," she screamed wildly, and Carlos rolled her over so he was on top and hammered home his seed.

Rosalee was so noisy he didn't hear the footsteps.

He barely felt the pain.

All he saw was black.

Something cold was splashed on his face and he came to. "What? What? What happened? Rosalee?"

"Ohhh, Carlos," she purred.

He blinked to clear his vision and saw Rosalee on the bed with a strange man between her legs. "Rosalee?"

"Carlos," she groaned and bent her legs.

"That's not me, Rosalee," he yelled and struggled, finding himself tied to a chair. "Hey, what's happening? What are you doing? Rosalee, snap out of it."

"She won't."

He looked up at the voice to his right. It belonged to a man whose face was covered in a weird Halloween mask.

"We gave her too much blow for her to snap out of it."

"What the fuck? Rosalee," Carlos yelled. "Rosalee, snap out of it, that's not me. That's not me."

"That's not me," Rosalee sing-songed. "Carlos..." Her legs were wide to give him passage, and he felt good inside of her. The room spun in every shade of every colour imaginable. Carlos sucked her breast, licked her neck and buried himself in her mouth.

"Rosalee, that's not me. You're being raped." He struggled with his bonds, his splitting headache, and the crazy scene before him.

"Rape?" the man beside him asked. "Do you see rape? She thinks it's you. She's making love to her man."

With fear and panic rising in his throat, Carlos

struggled to stand, but his head was making him weak, and sick, and unsteady. "Rosalee." What the hell was going on? "Rosalee." He weakened.

The man came with final grunting thrusts and rolled off. "Your turn." He stood up, zipped up, and looked down at Rosalee. "Fucking good."

The other man unzipped and got on, but he was rougher, faster, biting her breasts and neck, making her cry out in pain, or what pain she felt.

"Ow, Carlos, that hurts," she cried, gripping the man's jacket.

"Shut up, you whore. If you can take it from him, you can take it from me."

"Rosalee," Carlos yelled again. "That's not me, hey—"

The second man grabbed his shirt. "You shut your mouth."

Carlos struggled, but the man cracked him on the head. Dizziness came upon him. "Ugh, stop...stop..." In a daze, he watched the man finish up and roll off. After zipping up his pants, he picked up a small black kit from the bedside table and removed an already prepared syringe.

"What...what are you doing?" Carlos slurred through blurry vision.

"Dealing," the man said, and injected it into Rosalee's arm.

"Wait, no," Carlos yelled, but was hit over the head. All went black...

His eyes slowly blinked open.

He was lying sideways on the floor.

He tried to move his arms. They were no longer

tied to the chair, and he sat up. His brain wasn't functioning properly, but he saw enough to know Rosalee was dead, and he was in her house.

The sirens snapped him to attention. "Fuck!" He climbed to his feet and took another look at the woman. Drug paraphernalia, cocaine, needles, mirrors. They were all over the bed. "Oh, Rosalee…"

The sirens got louder.

"I gotta…Rosalee," he muttered. "Ugh, my head." He grabbed it to stop the pounding. "Rosalee," he wailed.

The sirens got louder.

He stumbled out of the room and through the lounge. "What…when…" The house was a mess. Furniture tipped over, magazines and pillows tossed everywhere. Stumbling for the front door, he could hear the sirens coming down the road. "Fuck!" He turned and stumbled out the back glass doors, onto the patio, and into the yard. "Fuck!"

The sirens stopped out front.

"Fuck!" Stumbling off the terrace, he crashed through the side fence into the neighbour's yard. "Fuck!" He held his head.

"Come quickly," a female voice said, and arms pulled him up and half dragged him through a side door, upstairs, and into a bedroom. "Stay there. I'll deal with this." She closed the door and went downstairs to watch the hubbub next door.

Police swarmed the house, the yard, her yard, the street. For an hour she watched them search and stand and talk before they knocked on her door.

"Yes." She stood before two detectives.

"I'm Detective Star, this is Detective Drew. We want to talk to you about what's happened next door," the tall brute of a man with an old scar on the left side of his face running from his ear down his jawline to his chin said.

"And what's happened next door?"

"There's been an overdose and a potential murder."

"Well, then let me describe to you the two men I saw leaving the house by the back door." She gave them a description of the men, their car, and the time they had arrived and left.

"You have a great memory. How'd you remember all that?" Star asked.

"I'm a photographer. I have a very visual memory."

"And your side fence? What happened there?"

"A gardening accident, yesterday."

"Do you know who owns the car out front of next doors?"

"My guest. There were cars in front of my house, so the only place left for him to park was in front of the house next door."

"Then we need to talk to your guest."

"He's not well and is sleeping at the moment."

"Then we'll have to catch up with him later."

"Yes, you will."

The two brown-suited detectives stared at the elegant black woman in a vibrant red dress and large gold hoop earrings, not even figuring that she was lying to them.

She stared back and kept her expression neutral.

Carlos came to an hour later when something was

being dabbed on his forehead. He blinked and grabbed his head. "Ugh. My head."

"I have some aspirin and water," the woman said.

His eyes opened to see her on the edge of the bed, dabbing his forehead with a wet cloth. "Who… what…?" He tried to focus, but the pain in his head was too much.

"Take the aspirin and rest. I'll get you something to eat." She left him alone and went downstairs, catching glimpses of the police next door while she made sandwiches. She took them upstairs and placed the plate on the bedside table. "Now." She took a seat in the chair next to the window. "Let's discuss the situation. Two men pulled up to the back of the house, walked through the back gate, put masks on, and entered the house by the back door. You arrived half an hour later through the front door. There was feminine screaming amidst, I'm sure, acts of lovemaking, and then the two men left, doing everything in reverse. And then you stumbled out as sirens wailed and you stumbled into my garden through the fence. I got you inside as the police turned up. An hour later two detectives told me a girl is dead, overdose or possible murder. Now…" She glanced from the window to him. "Tell me your side of it."

Carlos sat on the side of the bed and finished off the water. "Who are you and why should I incriminate myself? I should go." He stood up, but the dizziness made him sit back down.

She smiled. "I am Aneeka Ne Masta, world-famous photographer who has a shoot with you, Carlo Stefan, the hottest, newest porn star, on Wednesday. As luck would have it, I have proof that you were not the only one there and I have already given the police a description of the two men and their car. But…" She glanced outside. "They have probably checked your car's licence plates and discovered who you are and that you have been what…dating my next door neighbour."

Carlos swallowed the big fat lump in his throat. "Hadn't thought of that."

"And if there are any other neighbours home, who knows what *they* told the police."

"Fuck!" Carlos spat. "Fuck, fuck, fuck!"

"You could be in it up to your neck," Aneeka said. "So, tell me your side."

Carlos sighed. "I called Rosalee to see if she wanted to go to dinner and dancing, but she said to come over. She didn't sound good, so I raced over and found her door open and her naked on the bed. We had sex and then I was hit over the head." He got up and stretched before going over to stand beside Aneeka to look over the house. "When I came to, I was tied to a chair, and there was a man fucking Rosalee. She thought it was me, and I yelled at her that it wasn't, but…there was another man in a mask and he fucked her after the other man and then he…" He choked and turned away. "He got a needle and stuck it in her arm. Then I was hit over the head. I came to, heard sirens, found myself untied and Rosalee dead. Her place had been turned over. There was drug shit everywhere. I stumbled out the back because the cops were coming in the front. I fell into a fence, I think…

was that yours?" He stared down at the amazing-looking woman in the chair. She nodded. "I have a photo shoot with you this week?"

"Yes." She stood up. "I don't suggest using your car, they may have it bugged. Wait until dark and Harry will come and pick you up. I'll call him."

He stopped her at the doorway. "What if I need to prove I didn't do this? If they've already checked my car, they'll know I'm not a guest here, but the man Rosalee fucked occasionally. Can you prove others were there?"

"Of course, Mr Stephanopoulos. I'm a photographer. I took pictures." She left to call Harry who sent his chauffeur in an ordinary sedan to pick Carlos up at nine that night.

After turning off the lights, Aneeka ushered Carlos out the back door, through her gate, and into the open door of the sedan, all under the cover of darkness.

Carlos got to Harry's half hour later and spilt the whole story.

"There were TV crews and cops and people gawking," Harry bellowed.

"I know, I saw them."

"And what the hell were you doing there?" Harry stalked around his office.

"I called her to see if she wanted to go to dinner and she insisted I come over and it all went to shit." Carlos paced in the opposite direction so they crossed paths in the middle.

"Fuck, Carlos. You sure as fuck know how to get yourself into trouble, don't you?" Harry sucked his cigar as he walked.

"They'll know that's my car sitting in front and wonder why I haven't gone anywhere."

"You'll have to go and get it yourself."

"But what do I say if the cops ask?"

They stopped pacing in the middle.

"We'll have to think of something. Aneeka lives there, so we'll say you were visiting to talk about the photo shoot."

"But what if someone saw me go into Rosalee's?"

Harry blew smoke in Carlos's face. "We'll say she wasn't home and you went next door to talk."

Carlos nodded and waved the smoke away. "Could be reasonable. But what if someone's watching and I don't go and get it? Or ask why I didn't go next door when they turned up because I had been there and they turn up then they want to know why I didn't care enough to go next door and find out," he rambled. He was as scared as he had been in Greece.

"Well." Harry puffed. "We could say you did drugs together and then wandered next door to Aneeka's, but you passed out on the couch or something."

"Yeah, yeah." Carlos paced again. "And I'll walk out tomorrow and cry and pretend that I've just found out and stare at the house and take off, but I'll have to get back there to make it look believable in case the cops are watching." He shrugged. "Then if they pick me up it will look credible."

Harry nodded. "Then back to Aneeka's you go."

And at four past four in the morning, with lights off, Carlos sneaked back into Aneeka's house and waited until morning for the performance.

"No, no," he shouted and slammed out the front door, racing down the path and next door to Rosalee's. "No," he wailed as Aneeka came up and comforted him. "No." He collapsed onto the doorstep as the two detectives came up.

"And you're Carlos Stephanopoulos," Detective Star said, flashing his badge. "And you're under arrest."

"For what?" Aneeka questioned. "For being upset that a girl he dated has died? He didn't even know until this morning."

"Yeah." Star gave her the once over. "Strange, that. And you just *happened* to have conveniently seen two other men enter and leave the house."

"I did."

"Like we can take your word for it when you've been harbouring a criminal."

"Hardly a criminal." Aneeka stood. "A client. I am doing a photo shoot with him this week and he came over to discuss it, but passed out. And yes, smartass," she sassed the detective. "I can prove there were two other men there because I have photographs."

That wiped the smirk off Star's face and he exchanged glances with Drew. "Well, oh—"

"Yes," she interrupted. "I know. That's why I developed them yesterday and was going to give them to you at the station today. Now, are you still going to arrest Mr Stephanopoulos and on what grounds?"

Neither man liked being sassed by a woman, let alone a Negro woman. Who the hell did she think she was?

"Actually," Drew jumped in before Star could say anything. "We should get Mr Stephanopoulos's side of the story." He flipped open his notebook. "Mr Stephanopoulos." He looked down at Carlos who sat sobbing on the step. "Were you here yesterday?"

He gulped. "Ye-yes."

"At what time?"

"I don't know. Lunchtime or after."

"And what were you doing here?"

"I had called Rosalee to see if she wanted to go to dinner, but she demanded I come over here."

"She demanded?"

"Yes."

"What did you do?"

"I got in my car and drove over."

"About what time?"

"I don't know."

"What then?"

"The door was open, so I went in and called her name. I found her on the bed, naked. She wanted sex, so we had sex." He shrugged.

"And did you have any drugs?"

He winced. He had never taken drugs in his entire life and wasn't about to start.

"Well?"

"Yes," he lied.

"What?"

"A line of coke."

"That was it?"

"Yes."

"Then what?"

"Then Rosalee passed out, and I stumbled around a bit and went out the back. I found Aneeka's address in my wallet and realised she was next door so I went over and we talked about the photo shoot this week."

"How long for?"

"What?"

"How long did you talk for?"

Carlos shook his head. "Don't remember. I think I passed out."

The detectives turned their attention to Aneeka.

"Yes, he did and didn't wake up until about six this morning. That's when I told him about what he'd missed out on, and he told me his girlfriend lived there."

"Girlfriend?"

"We've dated about a month or so." Carlos wiped his face. He was done. "Can I go now? I need to get to work."

"And what do you do?"

"I'm an actor and writer."

"And drug-head by the look of it," Star said.

Carlos's face flamed with the fury.

"We'll get in touch with both of you if we have any more questions," Drew said. "Now, about those photos."

"Can I go?" Carlos climbed to his feet.

"Yes."

Carlos thanked Aneeka and made it to his car as she led the officers back to her place for the photos. He got in, took a deep breath, glanced at the house, and drove away.

*****

"You're damn lucky Aneeka took photos of those men coming and going. At least they have other suspects to look into so the heat should be off you for a while." Harry paced back and forth in his office. He'd just reamed Carlos out for ten straight minutes. "What *is it* with you and trouble?"

Carlos was deflated. He sat slumped on Harry's couch, having gone straight home from Aneeka's for a shower and shave, and then headed for Harry's.

"What the hell am I going to do with you?" Harry stopped to stare down at him. "Maybe I should keep you under lock and key."

"He could stay here," Harriet suggested from her position next to Carlos.

"Or maybe I can get you a bodyguard," Harry suggested.

Carlos looked up. "A bodyguard? I don't know if-"

"At least until this garbage has died down," Harry argued.

"But—" Carlos started.

"No buts!" Harry was definite.

"He has a nice butt," Harriet piped up.

"*Not now*, Harriet. No buts. You *will* get a bodyguard when you're out and maybe a guard to sit out front of your house at night. And *don't even think* of sneaking out, or seeing a girl, or screwing anyone, because it ain't on!"

"I wish he'd screw me."

"*Harriet, for the love of God,*" Harry told his wife.

Carlos stood. The two Harrys made him uncomfortable sometimes, especially the way they leered at him like meat. "I'm gonna go home. When's the photo shoot with Aneeka?"

"Wednesday, and don't miss it. You'll have a bodyguard on your way out."

Carlos nodded wearily. "Right. Will you be there?"

"Of course. I never miss Aneeka's photo shoots."

"Okay, see you then." Carlos walked outside with Harry yelling something about *'follow him, sit outside his apartment, you're his bodyguard now,'* and then a tall, short-shaven guy dressed all in black followed him out to his car. "Ah, you're…"

"Tony Vega, bodyguard."

"Okay. Are you coming with me?"

"Got my own car."

"Right." He drove off with his bodyguard tailing every move, unaware *he* was being tailed by another car.

✱✱✱✱✱

On Wednesday, Carlos showed up bright and early for his first photo shoot. He'd been in the business a few months, but had never had his photo professionally taken, and was looking forward to Aneeka taking them. Checking up on her previous work, he'd loved what she'd done. Everything from celebrities to porn stars, to landscapes; there were no bounds to her creativity.

His outfits were already waiting for him which made it easy to deal with. So he dressed and got hair and make-up done.

Aneeka turned up with her posse and set to work telling the crew where things needed to go and where she wanted Carlos to pose. After an hour she called everyone to attention. "All right, everyone, let's get to work. Carlos, get yourself into your cabana." She placed him where she wanted him. "And you are holding up well?" she asked quietly while she tucked his hair behind his ears and adjusted his top to show more flesh.

"As well as can be expected. You know Harry's given me a bodyguard?"

"So I heard." She tweaked his nipples so they protruded through his skin-tight tank top. He raised a brow. "We need you on display," she said smoothly. "You can do the rest." She nodded at his crotch. "Hard and penetrating. Okay, everyone, let's get to work."

For the next half hour, she directed Carlos in the cabana, from seducing the camera, to removing his clothes, to displaying his manhood with a towel hanging from it. She called time, and they moved on to the next set.

Carlos posed holding meat, in his uniform, out of his uniform, and only in his apron. They broke for lunch and Aneeka pulled him aside. "I gave the photos to the police. They were still quite surprised that I had taken them. I told them it's not often that strange men break into people's yards and enter the back door then leave hours later. Besides, my studio faces that way and I saw everything. I even sneaked out for a picture of their car while they were inside." She sipped a vodka and lemon.

"That could have been dangerous." Carlos knocked back a shot of tequila.

"Yes." She smiled. "But I have done more dangerous things than taking a photo of a car. Besides, all I had to do was step out of my own gate. Have you heard from the police again?"

"Not yet." He glanced across the crowd of movie and photo crew. "And hopefully, I won't. But knowing *my* luck with women and strange men, it will keep happening. I think I'm cursed."

"Cursed?" She arched a brow.

Carlos grinned. "Let's hope it doesn't happen a third time."

"Let's," Aneeka agreed. "Okay, everyone, back to work."

They spent the afternoon doing casual shots of Carlos in and by the pool, making sure to get him wet for full effect. Lounging and listening to music, drinking at the bar came next, and then they finished off for the day with sunset shots to take advantage of the smouldering rays as they lit up his tan and gorgeous blue eyes.

As they packed up after the shoot, the police turned up to speak to Carlos. They glanced around Harry DeVille's palatial home as they were led into the lounge.

"Detectives, we meet again," Aneeka said as she laid her camera in her bag. She always packed her own equipment to make sure no one damaged or dropped it.

"Ms Ne Masta." Detective Star nodded. "What a coincidence that you should be here when we want to talk with Mr Stephanopoulos again."

"It's not a coincidence, Detective," she replied smoothly. "You knew full well we were having a photo shoot. We told you on Monday."

Star moved uncomfortably at having been called out. "Yeah, well, it's a good thing you're here too; it will save us the trouble."

"Trouble with what, Detective?" she asked.

"Coming out to see you, Ms Ne Masta."

"And why would you need to see me again?" She zipped up her bag.

"Because we've spoken to some more witnesses…"

"And what witnesses would they be?" Aneeka asked. "Are they any better than me? Did they supply you with descriptions and photos and a car license plate?" She watched their uneasy expressions. "Well?"

"No," Detective Drew replied. "But they gave us other details like what time Stephanopoulos arrived and how long he was gone."

"As I told you—" Carlos started.

"Yeah, we get it, big boy," Star interrupted. "You fucked, snorted, and stumbled next door, but what we find funny is…" He stepped over to Carlos and poked his pen in his chest. "Is that *no one* saw you stumble over to Ms Ne Masta's." He aimed his pen at her. "Or do you want to tell us what really happened to that side fence of yours?"

"As I said—"

"Yeah, yeah, gardening accident." Star paced back and forth between them. "See, I get the feeling that the two of you are hiding something from me, from us." He waved his pen between him and Drew. "Now." He stopped. "Tell me I'm wrong."

"Detective." Aneeka stood straight and tall. "We have told you everything there is to tell. I gave you a description of the men and provided you with photographs. We have told you that Carlos was at my place because we were discussing *this* photo shoot." She waved an arm toward the gear still remaining. "That you can clearly see we have finished. Ask anyone here. We've been shooting all day. Now, I am going home to develop my photos. You know where I live if you want to continue harassing me." She nodded. "Detectives, Carlos." She gathered her bags and left with her staff, passing Harry on her way out.

"What in fucking hell are you doing in my house?" he bellowed as he walked down the steps into the lounge room. "I said…"

"We heard what you said." Detective Star put up his hand. "We came to talk to Mr Stephanopoulos."

"Not without a lawyer you don't," Harry snapped. "Now get out of my home."

Star went to open his mouth.

"Out." Harry pointed to the door. "Now."

With a disgruntled last glance at Carlos, they left.

"Now you." Harry pointed at Carlos. "Get home and stay there until shooting next week, your bodyguard's going to be there twenty-four hours a day, seven days a week, to stop these fuckers from getting to you. Now go."

Carlos reluctantly left and drove straight home, his bodyguard following.

So did the man in the dark sedan. He stopped at

the phone booth to call his boss and was told to wait to see if Carlos was in for the night and if so, then to go to the photographer's house and do his job. He got in the car and drove to Carlos's and waited until ten p.m. He didn't get out of his car; he didn't want to be noticed by the bodyguard sitting in his own car outside. Once it was obvious Carlos wasn't going out, he drove to Aneeka's house and waited until everyone's lights went out then quietly alighted from his car and made his way to the back yard.

*****

During his confinement, Carlos worked on new ideas for scripts and handed them to Harry when he turned up for the new movie. It was the second meat shop movie they were filming, and once again he'd written it. He was full of ideas and had gotten them down on paper, even drawing little layouts for how sets should look.

Harry read them over in his office while Carlos hit the set.

Today he was working with ethnic beauty Giselle Boudoir. She had a riot of curls tumbling down her back that matched the riot of curls between her legs. She was playing a foreigner visiting Greece. She was in need of meat…

They took their positions…

"And…action."

Giselle walked through the door wearing a see-through white dress and nothing underneath.

"Well, hello," Carlos murmured. "May I interest

you in some…meat…?"

Gisele stared dumbstruck by the golden god before her. "Well, I…"

Removing his apron, he came round the counter. "Let me show you today's specials?" He led her to the window display where half a dead cow resided. "It is all *meat…*" Carlos seduced. "From *every* angle."

Giselle licked her lips and put a hand on his chest. "And are *you* all meat?"

Carlos ripped off his uniform. "See for yourself!"

"Oh." She blushed. *"Oh, I need that meat."*

"Of course you do." He ripped open her dress, threw her backwards over the meat, and, spreading her legs, thrust inside.

Her head was lying amidst the remains of the cow, as gross as it was, and she was tilted at an angle so everything was on show in the window. Her breasts jiggled, her arms flailed above her head, her curls splayed across the animal and she groaned in pleasure. He stopped. "Oh, God," she groaned.

"Oh, God indeed," Carlos agreed as he pulled out, pulled her off the meat, turned her around and entered from behind.

She was grasping the meat in front of her, groaning, breasts on display for the camera. It was all a part of the porn. Tits and pussy and cock and mouth, nothing else mattered except those four things. And as long as the cameras zoomed in on female tits and mouth and pussy, and threw in a few cock shots to make women happy and men jealous, then the work was easy enough to do.

And it sold a motza!

When Carlos made her scream, it was over.

The *fantasy* was over.

He pulled out, donned his uniform while she adjusted her dress, and once again he offered her meat. Just as if sex had never happened.

And that was that.

"And…cut, print, good job." Andy Merkin, the director, was a dirty old man…more in his perverse sense of pleasure, not his age. He was forty-five and had started from the ground up in the movie industry, but became fed up when he wasn't getting the directing gigs he wanted. That's when he'd met Harry. Harry had seen something he'd done and offered him a job. Now he was making three times more than other movie directors and was getting to pursue his perverse passion on the side.

Sex, drugs and porn movies. It suited Andy down to a T. He got off on watching the sex scenes, as did the other men working there, got to score with a few of the actresses, and met bigwig TV stars, celebrities, and other actors at parties and nightclubs. This world suited him down to a T all right. T for tits. T for tongue. T for take it up the nose or the ass. Either way, it suited Andy Merkin perfectly.

Now his bulging erection showed he'd been turned on, as did a few other bulging pants. He needed to relieve himself and sneaked off to a quiet corner in another room with Suzy, Harry's maid, for a quick back end fuck over a chair. When he was done, he put it in his pants and left the room, and she straightened her uniform and pocketed the fifty bucks he'd given her.

She didn't like being treated like a piece of meat, dear old Suzy Q, as she was known. But at thirty-five she still looked good and had big tits and a big ass that could take a man like a champ. Plus she had a five-year-old son to raise so the money came in handy. How else could she get fifty bucks for five minutes' work? And back to work she went, servicing five more men in the next half hour, earning herself another two hundred and fifty bucks. Score! Three hundred bucks in one day and off the books paid her way through life, and she wasn't about to give it up. Besides, it was only an hour or so once a week. She could deal with that. Couldn't she?

Andy got to work in the editing booth while Harry and Carlos went over the photos from Aneeka's shoot.

"We're definitely using this one, and that will be a poster, that will be on the cover, that will be..." His imagination drifted off as he stared at a photo of Carlos in the pool, upper torso out of the water, his wet t-shirt plastered against his muscular chest, his hair in wet tendrils, his eyes penetrating into the souls of every woman, man, and child who dared lay eyes on them. "We're definitely using this one."

"Those are great photos." Carlos placed them in order. Cabana shots, meat shop shots, pool shots. "I've never done a photo shoot before, but that was well worth it."

Harriet came in with coffee and looked at the photos. Seeing the shots where Carlos was fully naked, she sighed. "If only I could get a taste of that sausage," she murmured. "Am I too old for you dear? You fucked Connie and didn't have a problem." She turned to see a surprised and uncomfortable Carlos slouched on the couch.

He reddened and sat up. "Um, Connie wasn't my boss."

"*I'm* not your boss. I'm only his wife." Harriet sat beside him.

"And I'm not about to go near you." Carlos got to his feet. "Harry, what did you think of the scripts?"

"Great, fantastic." Harry waved his cigar around. "And you'll get full writing credits on them as you will with the meat shop movies. That's why we can now give you a raise and your name will be on the boxes when the videos come out."

"And the movie posters and trailers?"

"And the posters and trailers! Now, what do you think about the Golden God idea? I see you floating down in a white loin cloth to bed the Greek women at your beck and call."

"Corny," Carlos said. "But I'll see what I can do with it."

"Good, good." Harry puffed. "Now I've spoken to a lawyer, and he said our story was a good one. By you admitting to going there and having sex, but lying about doing drugs and then remembering Aneeka lived next door, that should cover any evidence of yours that they find. But the cops are suspicious about the fence, even though Aneeka covered that, and they're suspicious about you being out of it for so long. But right now, they can't charge you with anything without proof, and since Aneeka provided them with two other potential killers, you should be okay for a while."

"And he needs to be; the porn awards are next week and he's been nominated for best newcomer," Harriet said.

"Already?" Carlos asked. "I thought they were months away and I didn't stand a chance?"

"Next week," Harry said. "And the ballots closed a week after your first movie came out, so we just scraped in. You're a shoo-in to win."

Carlos grinned. "I'm up for a porn award?"

"Yep, my boy." Harry got up and slapped him on the back. "You're up for an award."

"Will we be going?" Carlos asked. "What about everything that's going on?"

"You leave that to me—" Harry was interrupted by the phone. "Yes."

"Harry," Aneeka's panicked voice came down the line. "I've been broken into and my place has been trashed."

"What do you mean broken into? Don't you have security locks?"

"Of course, and I put my valuable things in the safe when I travel for a job, but someone still trashed it. Equipment, my photos, furniture, art, everything's been trashed."

"Have you called the police?" Harry asked as Carlos and Harriet gathered around, anxious to find out what had happened.

"Of course, they're on their way, but Harry, what if this has to do with what happened next door?"

"Don't consider that until you get some idea from the cops," Harry said. "Get your timeline together, your insurance papers, and anything else they may need. I'll get my private investigator onto it. Call me back after they're gone." He put the phone down and explained what had happened to Aneeka.

"Jesus!" Carlos said. "Do you think it has anything to do with Rosalee? Those men? What if they found out Aneeka took photos of them and trashed her place looking for them?" He paced back and forth. "What if they trash *my* place?"

"What do you have that they would want?" Harry asked.

Carlos thought about it and shook his head. "Nothing."

"Unless they do it to plant evidence," Harry went on. "Get your butt back to your place, Tony will go with you and search for anything that might be incriminating. Go." He ushered Carlos out the door and let Tony know what to do. "Stay on him like glue. Call me." He sighed and sat beside his wife on the couch. "That boy may make us big bucks, but he comes with a bucket load of trouble."

"Yes," Harriet agreed, swirling her pearls. "I wish he would let me deal with some of that trouble."

"Harriet," Harry snapped. "Must you *always* talk about fucking the boy? He's young enough to be your son."

"Aren't they all," she declared. "It's not as though I don't know about fucking, Harry. That's how you met me. I became your first porn star."

"And you were good at it until I decided to marry you."

She cocked a thin grey brow. "Are you saying I wasn't any good *after* you married me?"

Her tight lips and prim grey pantsuit were a turn off for him. "For a while." He got up and busied himself with the photos of Carlos.

"Well…" She stood up. "It's not like it stopped *you* from dipping your pen in the ink. I've had to put up with *that* all these years. So why shouldn't *I* get the pen dipped?" she huffed and stormed out the door.

"Because he's our best asset," Harry yelled. "And he clearly doesn't want you." He mumbled the rest under his breath. "Clearly doesn't want me either. Best to leave that boy to what he does best."

*****

Aneeka didn't wait for the police. She grabbed her camera that she'd had with her, loaded new film and took her own photos. She photographed every room that was trashed, the door locks, and the studio. She took photos of her smashed belongings, artworks, pictures, and documented it all down on paper, writing out a list of what was missing or broken. She checked her safe. All contents safe and accounted for.

The cops turned up an hour after her call.

"I would *hate* to have been injured," she said. "I would be dead waiting for you to turn up."

"Except you weren't harmed, so you're not dead," Detective Star muttered as he and Drew stalked around the house. "And when did you discover there had been a break-in?" He looked down at the floor to see he had stepped on a painted canvas. "If there *was* a break in."

"Do you think I did this myself?" Aneeka's anger rose. "That I trashed my own belongings and expensive photo equipment for the fun of it?" she snapped. "Let me tell you something, Detective Star, you are *not* very good at your job."

"And let me tell *you* something, *Ms* Ne Masta…" He stepped in to lean over her. "I find it highly suspicious that barely a week after your neighbour overdoses and her boyfriend crashes through your fence your house is broken into and trashed—"

"I told you—"

"Yeah, yeah." His temper simmered. *"Gardening* accident." He went nose to nose with her. "I know what you keep saying, *Ms* Ne Masta, but it doesn't jibe with other accounts and now this." He spread an arm out. "Where were *you* when this was happening?"

Aneeka hadn't blinked while standing toe to toe with Star. "I was away on a shoot all weekend. I got back this morning and immediately called the police who *chose* to take their time getting here. Now, I don't know if this is related to what happened next door, it could just be that they saw I wasn't home and broke in. That is up to *you* to determine."

Star hated the fact that a Negro woman so determinedly stood up to him, and he didn't give a flying shit if she was some world-renowned photographer or not. She was still a Negro.

"I see it in your eyes, Detective," Aneeka said. "Your ancestors owned slaves and you hate women, especially *black* women, standing up to you." She boiled inside, but remembered to stay calm, something she had to learn how to do many years ago. "I feel sorry for you, Detective."

He blanched at a black woman telling him she felt sorry for him.

"Sorry that you cannot move with the times like other people."

Now *his* blood boiled. "Who the hell are you to tell me that, you nig—"

"Star!" Drew yelled and grabbed the arm that had risen to hit the woman in front of them. He'd never seen his partner so riled up over a woman, even a black one, and was shocked that he'd raise a hand to one. "Calm down," he said.

Aneeka hadn't even flinched. "Yes, *Detective* Star, calm down, or you might give me a reason to file a complaint of harassment and assault on you."

Star launched himself at her, but Drew got in the way. "Let me go, get out of my way, Drew."

Drew shoved him backwards out the door of the studio, all the way downstairs and out the front door.

Star made racial slurs all the way and insinuations that she was involved with Carlos Stephanopoulos and the suspicious death next door.

The other officers stood in shock, glancing at each other, not knowing what to do. But Aneeka gave them no choice. Taking a deep breath, she said, "All right everyone, have you finished? I need to talk to my insurance officer next. Do you have everything you need?"

The officers took her lead and nodded, leaving her to repair her broken house. Once they were gone, she heaved a sigh of relief and slumped against the door, but saw the mess she'd have to clean up. Dear God, what was she up to her neck in? Did it have to do with next door? If they were after photos, then why not simply go through the studio? Why trash the whole house? Since the whole house was trashed, was it normal crooks looking for a place to do over?

Someone knocked on the door and she jumped. "Oh." Peering through the peephole, she saw it was her insurance broker. She didn't know what she was going to do, but it would have to wait.

*****

Carlos sped back to his apartment with Tony close behind. They made record time, and raced up the stairs before Tony stopped Carlos so he could open the door.

"We need to be careful in case they've trashed your place too." He motioned for Carlos to step back and pulled a small black revolver from the band of his pants. Slowly, carefully, he put his army and C.I.A. training into use. Pushing open the door, he peered through the gap. Seeing no one, he moved the door back, and with his pistol pointed, entered the apartment. Seeing and hearing no one, he silently moved through the two bedrooms, bathrooms and back into the lounge and kitchen. He checked all the windows and balcony doors. When he was satisfied there were no wires, bugs, or explosives, he motioned for Carlos to enter and closed the door behind him. "Sit at the dining table," he instructed. "I'm going to take this place apart."

Carlos nodded and took a seat while Tony explored every nook and cranny, coming up with bloodied drug paraphernalia tucked away behind the toilet in the master suite. He searched the whole place from top to bottom and found a bag of drugs, some bloodied material, and photos of Carlos and Rosalee passed out on her bed before she was killed. He placed them on the table in front of Carlos who started to talk, but Tony quickly put his finger to his lips to silence him.

He went to the phone on the kitchen bench, unscrewed the bottom half to check for bugs and found one. After twisting the cap back on, he called Harry. "Hey, Harry, can you send Mike over to relieve me. I've got a hot date tonight and there are some things I wanna show her…if you know what I mean…"

Harry knew exactly what he meant. "Mike's on his way."

"Thanks, Harry." Tony replaced the phone in its cradle for a few moments before picking it up, unscrewing the cap and removing the bug. He put the phone back together and gathered everything, placing each piece into a coat pocket, so when he walked out it looked as if he had nothing. And if anyone *was* watching, they would think no one had found the incriminating evidence.

Mike arrived twenty minutes later and Tony walked

out to meet him.

"Mike."

"Tony. Hot date, man."

"Yep, gotta go and get ready."

"Make sure to get it up then."

"I plan on it."

Mike went inside and Tony left, driving back to Harry's. They studied the evidence on Harry's desk.

Harry tasted the drug. "Cocaine." He checked the pills. "Uppers." He looked at the photos. "She's drugged off her face."

"What do we do with it?" Tony asked.

Harry thought about it. "If I burn it, it might be needed somehow to prove his innocence."

"Or guilt."

Harry sighed. "Or guilt," he agreed. "But I just can't see him doing something like that. He's a good kid, really. If I keep it, it could be found and used against him."

"So, what do we do with it?" Tony asked again.

Harry paced the room. "Lock it up where no one will find it."

*****

The man in the car had watched Carlos arrive with the big bald guy right behind him. They'd entered, and an hour later another man had turned up, greeting the bald guy as he came out. They exchanged talk about a date and getting it up.

He hadn't gotten it up properly in months. It's not

that he hadn't tried. It's just that his boss kept him busy watching Carlos Stephanopoulos. Some big guy with a big dick who got it out a lot. *More than he did.* He didn't know why his boss wanted him watching some porn guy, only that he had to, and supposed his boss had some big plan for the newest porn star. And regardless of what his boss wanted, he'd gone out and seen the movies. He was bored. He'd needed something to do in what little spare time he had. So he'd sat in the movie theatre up the back, getting off to the movie as he was sure everyone else in the room was doing.

Regardless of the reason why he was watching Carlo Stefan, the guy was gorgeous and had a huge dick, and the women he fucked in the movie he'd imagined himself fucking in exactly the same way. After knocking a couple of young girls unconscious, he'd fucked them exactly the same way as Carlo did in the movie.

Of course, he wouldn't be able to do that if they were conscious. They wouldn't want him. They wouldn't even look at him. So he had to find alternative ways of having sex…without paying for it. He'd covered his face and burned the clothes he'd worn so they wouldn't find him even if they looked.

And then there was that pretty young thing called Rosalee.

His cock was hard just thinking about the girls he'd had, and he released it from its nylon prison. "Ah, that's better." It stood, slightly limp, slightly bent in the sun beating its way into the car, seeking release. But he held on, stroking, massaging, pretending he was Carlo

Stefan, ready to put his ten inch cock into some young thing's mouth. He felt the warmth of that mouth, the sucking and sliding, a mouth ever so greedy for what he had. For what it wanted. He felt himself peak and come, groaning, tilting his head back, and thrusting his crotch back and forth in the motions.

He sweated and groaned as the mouth sucked harder and he came again.

Tap tap tap tap.

"Oh, yes, tap away," he groaned.

Tap tap tap tap.

He moaned at the interruption and opened his eyes to see a police officer staring at him through the window.

Ah, fuck!

*****

Carlos stayed indoors until the following week when he filmed another movie and got ready for the porn star awards. Everyone had been partying hard at Harry's that day, and they all got dressed, drank, ate, fucked, and were merry right up until it was time to go.

Harry, Harriet, Carlos and Tony piled into Harry's limo, while everyone else piled into two others.

"So, my boy, turns out we're up for quite a few awards, including best cock, best script, best director, best actor, best newcomer, best actress…"

Carlos's eyes widened. "That's almost all of them."

"Yes." Harry grinned. "Almost all of them."

"What are these porn awards like then?" Carlos put

the window down a little and peered out into the night.

"*Big*, in more ways than one." Harriet giggled.

"Bulging," Harry added.

"Horny," Harriet continued.

"Yep, everyone's horny, hot and hard." Harry's grin grew larger. "It *is* the porn awards after all."

They cruised down Santa Monica Boulevard and slowed down to form a line of limos all waiting to deposit their guests at *The Pussycat Theatre* where the awards were held every year. They chatted until it was time to alight.

Harry stepped out first to thunderous applause and then helped Harriet. The two stood, waving to fans and cameras like some big movie stars, and then moved aside for the real star.

Carlos bounded out of the car waving, blowing kisses, and hearing fans scream wildly for him. Flashlights popped, men *and* women called for him, and one young man broke loose to come screaming toward him, lurching at him, grabbing him around the waist.

Tony did his job and quickly bent the man's fingers back to release his grip, then twisted his arm behind his back and pushed him into the waiting arms of security.

"Carlo, I love you," the young man screamed, tears pouring down his face. "I love you."

"Jesus," muttered Carlos, stunned at the attack. "You didn't tell me it was going to be like this." He pushed his hair back which made his fans scream louder.

Harry let out a great big thunderous laugh. "Carlos, my boy…" He put his arm around his shoulders. "You're a star now!"

With Tony following up the rear, Harry led Carlos and Harriet up the red carpet and into the theatre.

The red extended inside with carpet, velvet walls, disco balls, couches with feather boas and whips, mannequins with costumes of spikes and chains, not to mention sex toys liberally sprinkled around. They made their way past other stars into the auditorium and took their seats in the middle of the room. The theatre itself was full of old wood and velvet curtains, velvet covered chairs, and bright lights.

After ten minutes the lights dimmed, the curtain rose, and the annual Porn Star Awards began with a rousing musical act that performed while sucking dildos and blow up dolls. The disco ball lights twinkled, the speakers blared, and Carlos sat in stunned amazement.

Ackroyd Ackerman came out to present the first award to thunderous applause, waving to the audience. "Thank you, thank you. I love you, too." He was one of the oldest porn stars at forty-nine, but looked twenty-nine, and came with a twelve inch cock. He was one of the best in the industry.

"And the first award is…Best Male Newcomer to the industry. And the nominees are…" He read the names while footage of the actors rolled across the screen behind him. "Milos Pensuala, Archer Target, Bennon Frankme, Dale Rideher, what a great name that is, and last but definitely *not* least…Carlo Stefan."

The crowd went wild at every name, especially Carlos's.

"And the lucky winner is..." Ackroyd ripped the envelope open excitedly. "Carlo Stefan," he yelled and applauded wildly. He had a big thing for Carlo as he swung both ways and wouldn't mind giving it to him sometime. *I must ask him if he's interested in me,* he thought.

Carlos sat in shock as the crowd thundered around him, staring dazedly at the two Harrys.

"Go on, my boy, go and get your award." Harry pulled him up from his seat and Tony stood in the aisle, his eagle eye on the lookout as Carlos stumbled his way down the stairs and onto the stage to collect his silver penis award.

"Oh, wow." He accepted it from Ackroyd, who kissed him on the mouth. "Oh, um, oh, ah." Ackroyd let him go, and he turned to the microphone with a frown. "I..." He shook his head and glanced over the adoring audience. "I'm in shock....I...I never thought I'd be here in Hollywood receiving an award." He looked at it in his hand. *"A big silver penis award."* The crowd cheered. "For liking sex so much." More cheering. "I love women..." He threw a glance at Ackroyd. "I love acting, I love writing, I love being *with* women, and now I get paid to do all of it and you all get to see it."

"All ten inches," someone screamed from the crowd.

Carlos blushed. "Yes, about the size of this." He held up his award. "Thank you so much. Thank you." The hot Latin woman who had brought the award on stage led him backstage to be interviewed. He stood on a platform in front of cameras and reporters, answering questions while more awards were announced, including Andy Merkin for Best Director of the Cabana movie that was Carlos's first.

Carlos answered questions the best he could, but Tony soon stepped in and led him back to his seat as Best Producer was announced.

Harry won it for Cabana, and dragged Carlos on stage with him, huffing and puffing on his cigar to accept the award.

"Thank you, thank you. I couldn't have done it without this cock here." He pulled Carlos close. "Without it, I wouldn't be here this year. Thank you." They went backstage and were told to wait as Best Cock was being announced.

Ackroyd took to the microphone again. "And now…we come to my favourite award where I get to see if young Hollywood measures up to old Hollywood." He dropped his pants for all to see his twelve inch cock and read out the nominees to thunderous applause. "And the nominees for Best Cock are…Centurian Masters, Villa Vion, Richard Head, Marcos Du Mont and my personal favourite whose cock I can't wait to see in person is…Carlo Stefan…"

"Jesus," Carlos muttered as Harry slapped him on the back. "Is this guy for real?"

"Yes. And you…" Harry pointed at him. "Have to drop your pants out there and show them why you won Best Cock."

"I haven't won yet," Carlos said.

"Carlo Stefan!" Ackroyd yelled out.

"You have now, go show 'em." Harry slapped him some more, and Carlos walked out to a standing ovation of screams and wolf whistles. He waved and tried not to look at Ackroyd's cock hanging for all to see as he was presented with a gold penis award. Gold, for best cock.

God love Hollywood!

"Get it out, get it out, get it out," chanted through the crowd and Carlos embarrassedly glanced at Harry in the wings. He waved at him to drop his pants, and reluctantly, he placed the award on the small lectern and dropped his pants.

"Whoo," screamed through the crowd and he quickly pulled his pants back up. "Okay, okay, thank you for the adulation and the award. It's going on the bedside table." He waved and quickly left the stage. "*That* was embarrassing," he told Harry and went to keep walking, but was stopped.

"You're up for more awards in a minute."

Ackroyd went on to announce Best Actor, Carlos again, and Best Movie, Cabana, which Harry and Carlos both went on stage for. That was it for them, and they made their way back to their seats as the final performance came on stage.

"What now?" Carlos asked, hanging on to the three cocks in his hands.

"Now we go and party," Harry said and led the way out to their limo.

The club was already packed with people and had more outside waiting to get in. They were quickly led through the back door and made their way to the private roped off area. Alcohol was flowing, drugs were being snorted or injected, and sex was happening on the dance floor.

Roller-skating women delivered drinks; roller-skating men delivered the drugs. With the pulsating beat of the music and the twirling lights of the disco balls, Carlos found himself lost in the atmosphere and the alcohol.

The rest of the crew turned up followed by everyone else that had been at the awards. Men and women congratulated Carlos, and Ackroyd tried for a cock-off.

He pulled his out. "Come on, show me yours, let's compare."

Carlos backed away. "No thanks." He turned around to find himself in the arms of Vivian. "Viv." He picked her up and spun around to the beats of the music blaring at them from all angles.

"Well, hello there, Mr Best Cock. Tell me, is your award bigger than you?" She laughed as he put her back on her feet and slipped her arms around his neck, tossing back her long brown hair.

"Same size, I think." He laughed. "Where have you been? I haven't seen you in ages." He held her close and thrust against her as they swayed to the pounding music.

"I've been away, darling. Photo shoots in Paris, Milan, London, Tokyo." She hooked a leg up to his waist and thrust back.

His hands grabbed her and held her tight. "How

about coming to my place. We can spend the night together."

"After the trouble you've gotten yourself into? I'm not sure I'd be safe alone with you."

He frowned. "How do you know about it?"

"Harriet, darling."

The frowned deepened. "How about your place then? I miss you, Viv." He twirled her around and slid a hand between her legs to find she didn't have any panties on.

"How about here, darling," she said in his ear and slid a hand down to unzip his erection.

Under the tribal beating and dizzying lights, they made their way together on a rhythmic beat all without missing a step until the music slowed down and they remained joined through a slow dance with Carlos massaging her firm ass and Vivian clenching her well-trained womanhood. Their tongues entwined and they stayed that way for five more songs before reluctantly parting and walking up to their private party for a drink.

"Viv, how are you, my dear." Harry got up to give her a kiss.

"Good thanks, Harry."

"I see you've done some sampling of the Best Cock of 1977."

"Not the first time, Harry." Viv laughed.

"Guess not," he replied.

"We're gonna get a drink and go." Carlos came up with two champagnes.

"Not without Tony you're not," Harry said, and

Carlos noticed him standing nearby.

"A bodyguard? How very celebrity of you." Viv sipped her drink.

"I need to keep my boy safe now, don't I," Harry replied. "So, if you two leave, take him with you." He threw himself back into the melee.

Carlos downed his drink. "Ready?"

"Ready." Viv led him by the hand and they walked out into the quiet air of downtown L.A. Tony flagged their limo down, and they headed for Viv's luscious Hollywood Hills home where Tony did a perimeter check as they went in.

"Wow, great looking place." Carlos eyed the antiques and art on the walls, tables, and pedestals.

"I like expensive things." She led him to the enclosed backyard where the pool was lit, and the spa was already on. Slipping out of her dress she helped Carlos out of his suit and shirt.

He picked her up and dipped into her before dipping into the spa. Holding her up over the side, his long even strokes thrust her back and forth.

"Oh, God, oh, God, Carlos. Oh, God, I've missed this," she gasped as the hot bubbling water slapped against her ass.

He gave one last stroke and lifted her to him, delving into her mouth and tasting the champagne. It was so good to be with her again; a woman who wanted him for him and not because he could give it to her. He tasted her neck, her breasts, her nipples.

"Ugh," she groaned and tightened her inner sanctum, clenching him, keeping him there, and hardening him.

He sucked harder.

She clenched harder.

They came together.

Lying on a poolside lounge afterwards with a towel over them and more champagne inside of them, they stared up at the stars.

Carlos told her his side of everything and Viv offered her opinion. Then she told him everything she'd been doing, and they made love until the sun came up.

He stroked her soft, dewy cheeks. "I love you, Viv," he said.

She moved her head back in shock. "What?"

He laughed. "Don't panic. I've loved you since I was fourteen and you were on my bedroom walls. You're my dream girl. And then I met you, and you were everything I thought you were and then some. Beautiful, sassy, vibrant. Great in bed."

"And out of it," she quipped.

He laughed again. "And out of it." His fingers slipped down her throat to her breast and played with her nipple which hardened in an instant. "You're beautiful, and I love you. I just wanted you to know that. I don't expect anything from you, and you won't get anything else from me. Unless you want it. But I just wanted you to know." He kissed her lips before his mouth latched onto her erect bud.

She sighed. Completely relaxed, completely free, completely happy. "I love you too," she murmured and arched into his mouth. "Oh, God." She enjoyed the freedom she had with him. To be the sexual nymph she was. No other man had pleasured, pleased, or fulfilled her like he did, and she'd been so glad that Harriet had let her know about him. Because once she'd tasted him, she didn't want anyone else to occupy her pussy. It was for him and him alone, and she'd missed him terribly when she was away, not even realising he'd get personally involved with someone else. But he had and now more trouble had followed. Was he worth it considering how he filled her? Of course he was, but he was still so young. Sixteen years her junior. But then, they *were* in Hollywood where age doesn't matter, especially when surgery for looking younger was becoming big business. As long as he kept those ten inches up and at attention that was all she needed.

Cock.

Cock was all she needed. But the body it came with wasn't bad either. She wrapped her legs around that body as he entered her, sliding in like he owned the place.

She looked into his eyes. He owned her, every time. This place was his and his alone. No one else had been in it since him, and no one else would be in it after him. That's why he needed to stay. This place was his and his alone. Did she dare keep a younger man? It was not as though he needed her money. Did she dare keep a porn star for a lover? It's not like he fucked too many others outside of work. It had only been Rosalee, but that didn't last. No, there would never be another for her as long as Carlos Stephanopoulos fucked her senseless all night every night like now. Oh, God, oh, God, oh…God…

They slipped into a semi-conscious state and stayed that way all day, drifting in and out, making love, sleeping, lying in the sun, drinking in the pool, the spa, on the lounge. They stayed that way all day.

*****

Aneeka was in her studio looking at her recent photos. She hadn't seen or heard from Carlos, Harry, or the cops since the break-in and had wondered if they'd be back. The insurance company had her claim on the go, and she'd installed a better security system than the one she had.

She glanced out the window to the house next door. The police had come back and removed the tape. A company had come and cleaned it out of furniture, and any evidence of drugs, and now there was a for lease sign on the front. The rental company hadn't waited long. The poor girl wasn't in her grave yet.

She picked up her camera to give it a polish and made sure there was a film in it, then methodically went through each piece. Around midnight she went downstairs to make a cup of tea, a ritual she did every night if she was still awake at twelve.

Getting the kettle on the stove, she got a sachet of her favourite herbal tea out and placed it in a mug. While waiting for the water to boil, she went through the house making sure the windows were closed and the doors were locked. She noticed her neighbours had all gone to bed because the only lights on were hers and the street lights.

On hearing the kettle whistle, she poured water over the sachet and let the fumes waft up to her nose. Just the scent of it made her calm. Sitting at the table, she read a magazine and saw an ad for Carlos's new movie which featured one of her photos.

"He *is* gorgeous," she murmured and had been quite hypnotised by his blue eyes when taking the photos, especially the ones in the pool where his eyes were the focus. After finishing her tea and putting the magazines away, she saw her rubbish bin was overflowing and decided to take it out. She tied the bag up, unlocked the back door, and stepped onto her porch going over to the side fence where her bin was. *Better not forget rubbish day this week.*

The back light went out, and she turned at the sudden darkness, a chill creeping down her spine. "Damn light bulbs," she muttered. "There must be one that lasts longer than this." She hurried up the stairs, across the porch, and managed one foot in the door before she was grabbed from behind with one arm around her waist and one arm over her mouth with a rag that smelled sweet…sickly…sweet…

*****

Carlos managed to make it home the next day, even though he'd wanted to stay, but Viv had another shoot to go to in New York and needed to leave. So he'd stumbled through the house and out to the car that was now there with Tony behind the wheel.

"Tony, man. Have you been here the whole time?"

Carlos slumped into the back seat.

"No, sir. I was relieved and came back with this car. Home, sir?"

"Thanks, Tony."

Carlos rested his eyes behind black shades on the drive home and didn't take them off until he walked inside his apartment. Only then did he see the mess that lay before him.

"Tony," he yelled. "Tony."

Tony came hurtling through the door and saw the overturned dining set, lounge suite, broken prints, smashed glass and half-open balcony door. He whipped his gun out and stalked toward the other rooms.

Carlos waited.

"Clear. You'd better come see this."

Carlos followed the trail of destruction into his bedroom where he saw the upturned bed and strewn sheets. "What?"

"That." Tony pointed.

On the mess that was the bed lay a photo of Aneeka, bound to a chair and gagged with today's paper held under her face. The note that came with it read, *'We want the photos she took. We want you. Get us those photos and all negatives, or she dies. If you call cops, she dies. If you take off out of town, she dies. If you don't do as you're told, she dies. We want photos. We will call at 3:30 p.m. Tell anyone, she dies.'* The words were crudely written, the paper ripped from a ruled notebook.

"We'd better call Harry," Tony said.

*****

"What the fuck is happening here?" Harry bellowed. He paced across his office and back. "Your girlfriend gets killed, and now Aneeka is kidnapped all because of the photos. *What* photos?"

"Photos of Carlos's girlfriend's house and the two intruders," Tony stated.

"And now that means they're all combined." Harry was pissed. Pissed off that the golden Adonis he'd put so much money into was causing him so much trouble. "Is trouble your middle name?" he asked. "'Cause that's all you've caused me."

"I had nothing to do with this," Carlos yelled. "Aneeka took those photos, she told the cops those guys killed Rosalee. That had *nothing to do with me.*"

"Well, who are they and what do they want?" Harry continued.

"I don't know," Carlos yelled back. "I have no idea who they are, or what they want, or why they killed Rosalee. I...don't...know!" Carlos was frustrated and overwhelmed. His life had been turned upside down since that night in Mykonos, and now it was continuing. What the fuck was going on?

"What do we do?" Tony asked. He had stood straight and tall the whole time, not moving. Army training.

Harry paced. Harry puffed. Harry waved his hands in the air. "I don't know." He picked up the note and read it again. "Photos. They want photos. Where are those photos? What the fuck do they want them for?"

"Because they're photos of the men that killed Rosalee and tried to frame me for it," Carlos said. He wiped his face and leant against Harry's desk. "They don't want anyone knowing they were there."

"*Why* did she have to take photos of them?" Harry asked.

"And tell the police and give them copies," Carlos added. "I was there when she told them she had photos. It was the day after, and she gave them to them after I left."

"So, if anyone was still lurking around, they would know about them."

Carlos nodded. "Probably."

"And that's why her house was trashed," Tony added. "They must have been looking for them."

"Did she still have them?" Harry paused thoughtfully, puffing on his cigar. "She made copies to hand over but did she make more?"

"Don't know," Carlos said, crossing his arms. He'd been nothing but trouble, and now he was feeling guilty for bringing this upon everyone.

"But she should still have the negatives," Tony said. "Does she have a bank vault, a safety deposit, house safe? Does she keep personal stuff somewhere special?"

Harry thought. "I know she puts her valuable stuff in a safe in her home when she travels."

"Where is it?" Tony asked.

Harry thought some more. "In a small hidden room…" His eyes narrowed. "Between her studio and the…stairs. Under the stairs." He frowned. "Something to do with the stairs."

"Okay, here's the plan," Tony said, checking his watch. "It's twelve now. We'll go and search her house. Do you have a key or know if she leaves one out?"

"No, no, I have one for emergencies." Harry pulled out a huge keyring full of about a hundred keys from his desk drawer.

"Right, we'll go search and be back at Carlos's by three-thirty. Then we'll take the next step."

"What's the next step?" Carlos asked.

"Doing what they want," Tony said, taking the key Harry gave him. "What about an alarm system?"

"Ah," Harry faltered. "She had a new one installed, but if they got her, they probably cut it or something."

"Do you know the code, just in case they didn't?"

"Uh…" Harry paced again. "It's uh…uh…uh…" He tapped his forehead. "It's something to do with… 6547." He snapped his fingers. "6547."

"Right," Tony said. "Let's go, Carlos, we need to find those pictures." He started for the door but stopped. "What's the safe code?"

Harry shrugged. "Probably the same code. I think she uses the same one for everything."

"Not a very safe thing to do," Tony replied. "Come along, Carlos."

They drove to Aneeka's and walked up the stairs to the porch with Tony on guard for any strange vehicles or lurking strangers. He unlocked the door and stepped inside. The alarm pad blinked to his right and he quickly tapped the code in. Closing the door made it blink green.

"I'll check the place out first, see how they got her."

Tony went straight for the back door and found the light globe untwisted, and a pot plant knocked over. He walked over to the back gate and found it unlocked and a cut padlock on the ground. "Mmm," he mumbled.

Going back inside, he shut and locked the door, and they went upstairs to her studio. Tony measured walls and layouts and started pushing wall panels. He pulled objects, shifted prints and finally heard a click.

The wall panel slid aside, and they saw a small room with two huge safes, one on either side, that would have been neatly packed away under the stairs in the hallway.

"Nice," Tony said. "But which bloody one?"

Carlos hovered behind him. "Try both. It's one-thirty."

Tony got to work with the safe on his left and used the same code as the security system. It opened, and he quickly pored through the paperwork and small boxes. "No negatives." He closed the door and locked it then turned his attention to the second safe. Same code, same time to open it.

There were boxes of negatives neatly filed away by date. He quickly found the box, and they both checked through it, finding the right negatives in a few seconds.

"We've got them, let's go." Tony put everything back, and they hightailed it out of there and back to Carlos's not even noticing the two men following in a car.

One hour later the phone rang.

Carlos jumped. He'd been expecting it, but they had been sitting in silence so the sound was incredibly loud in such a small quiet room.

"Answer it," Tony said.

After taking a deep breath, and wiping his sweaty palms on his pants, Carlos picked up the phone. "Hello."

"Ah, Carlos Stephanopoulos himself," the voice said, the Greek accent coming through. "Do you have the negatives and photos?"

"Yes."

"Good. You're to take them to Venice Beach Pier. You are to go underneath and leave them in rubbish bin."

"What if I don't?"

"Then she is dead."

"Why are you doing this? Why did you kill Rosalee?"

"Because we were told to."

Carlos's eyes widened and he looked at Tony who was listening next to him. "What? What do you mean you were told to?"

"It doesn't matter, you need to leave the photos in bin under pier. Leave them and walk away. Go there now. Now, Mr Stephanopoulos, now and do not tell police."

The phone went dead.

Carlos breathed and stared at the phone in his hand.

"He didn't tell us if they'd let her go, though." Tony grabbed the phone and disconnected the call. "And that could be a problem." He called Harry. "They want us to deliver the photos to a bin under Venice Beach Pier, now. How fast can you get men down there... Right...

Right… Right…we're off." He replaced the phone. "Let's go."

"But they said tell no one," Carlos stated, following Tony out the door.

"They said don't tell the cops, Harry's men aren't cops." Tony bolted down the stairs with Carlos on his heels.

"We could get her killed," Carlos shouted, running after Tony to the car.

"Get in," Tony snapped. "And keep your bloody voice down." They sped off. "Look, they could kill her anyway whether they have the photos or not."

"God." Carlos ran a hand through his hair. "Why the hell is this happening?"

"Let's go over this," Tony said. "You get involved with Rosalee, then these thugs kill her and try to frame you, and when they find out photos were taken by the neighbour—"

"How did they find out, though?" Carlos butted in. "Really?"

"They probably kept an eye on Rosalee's house to see who came and went. If they spotted Aneeka talking to the cops and handing over photos, they may have looked into her, found out what she knew, put two and two together, and figured she may have seen something. So they grabbed her."

They pulled into the car park at the wharf. "Right, listen closely. You give me five minutes to get into position, and then get out and slowly go down to the bin and leave the package. Then get the hell out of there and back here. You got it?" He saw Carlos's stunned expression and grabbed his arm. "You got it?" he demanded, snapping him out of his trance.

"Yeah." Carlos swallowed the lump in his throat. "Yeah."

"Right." Tony opened the door and looked around. "Give me five minutes, check your watch."

It was ten past four.

Tony left to get into position, and after waiting five minutes, Carlos followed. Making his way down to the sand, he walked underneath the wharf and looked around for the bin. He found it, and placed the package inside. Glancing around, he had turned to go back when a sharp pain stabbed through his head, and all he saw was black.

"Quick, grab the photos," a man said and started dragging Carlos toward the water. "Have you got them?"

"Yeah."

"Then help me."

The two men quickly carried Carlos to the water where they had a small inflatable boat. They dumped him on board, revved the engine, and sailed away, glancing back to see Tony and several men running toward the water.

"We've been seen," one man said.

"And there are cops," the other said. "We said no cops."

They watched the cops take down Tony and roared off into the distance.

"What the fuck are you doing?" Tony yelled. "They've got a hostage."

"Yeah, yeah," Detective Star said, clicking the cuffs shut. "And what hostage would that be?" They started leading him up the sand toward the stairs.

"Aneeka Ne Masta," Tony spat. "You've just stuffed up a hostage negotiation." He struggled and managed to push Star away. "And now they have Carlo Stefan and you've got me in cuffs, you dick wank."

"Who do you think—" Star dived at him, but Drew held him back.

"What do you mean they have Ne Masta and now Stefan?" Drew asked.

"They kidnapped Aneeka Ne Masta because she'd taken photos of them coming and going from Rosalee's house. She fingered them, and they broke into her house looking for the photos. *They're* the ones who trashed her place, and they wanted Carlos to get them and deliver them."

"How did you get into her house? Did you have the damn code?" Drew asked.

"Yes," Tony sneered. "*And* we got the negatives. We were in the middle of the hand off when you dick wanks fucked it up. And now they have Stefan."

Star lurched at him. "Well, if you hadn't been lurking around maybe we would have caught the guys we've had under surveillance since we found out about them."

Drew got between them.

"You had them under surveillance?" Tony asked incredulously. "Then you know who they are and where they have Aneeka?"

"Of course we know where they are, but it's not like

we're gonna tell you," Star raved.

Tony roundhouse kicked him. "She could be dead because of you," he screamed and got taken down by ten cops as Drew helped Star to his feet. He was hauled away. "She could be dead because of you, Star. How's your boss gonna deal with one of his detectives letting the thugs keep a kidnap victim?" He was taken up to the van and shut inside.

"You okay?" Drew asked, gaping at Star.

"Just fine." He spat blood out. "Let's lock that prick up."

But an hour later, Star was left red-faced after a dressing down from his superior after *he'd* had a chat with Harry DeVille.

"*You knew* where they were and where they were going, but you didn't know they had a world-famous photographer under lock and key?"

"Um, no sir," Star muttered, shifting from one foot to the other.

"How goddamn incompetent are you, Star?" Captain Ward yelled, his veins popping out of his temple as his face turned red. "I should demote you." He thrust a finger in Star's face. "But I'll wait to do that *until* you have told Tony Vega everything you know about the two men in those photographs and *what you've done* with them under surveillance. You will tell him *everything* and then help him find Ms Ne Masta *and* Mr Stefan safe and sound." He looked from Star to Drew and back again. "*Both of you.* Is that understood?"

"Yes, sir."

"Good, now Vega is ex-army and C.I.A., and I trust *him*, not *you* right now, so you do what you're damn well told." Ward strode around his desk. "Get out."

The detectives hurried back to their desks to find Tony poring over paperwork.

"I want to know everything you know. Who are they, where they're from, and how long they've been here? What they eat, where they shit, and who they've fucked. If you don't know, find out," Tony said at the two brooding men. "Let's get started."

Star slumped into his seat, crossed his arms, and refused to talk.

Drew did it for him. "After we received the photos from Ms Ne Masta we tracked down their license plate but found it had been stolen two weeks earlier. As luck would have it, a man was picked up down the street from Stefan's getting himself off in his car. It was a different car than the one outside Ms Brentworth's place, but the man fitted the description. After he was charged with indecent exposure we put a tail on him. We've been tailing him and his partner since. From Stefan's place to Ne Masta's, back to their hotel, which we've checked into. They used aliases. The man we picked up is Dimitri Yustoff, of Greece. We have passports and driver's licences."

He handed the papers over. "But he's been using different names wherever he goes. We also tried to connect him with some assaults; three women, attacked by an unknown assailant. We wondered if it might be one of them. He was seen masturbating at a Carlo Stefan movie a few weeks back."

"Who hasn't," Tony said, looking at the photos of the man. "Do you know when they could have taken Aneeka?" He continued dealing with Drew.

"In the early hours of this morning," Drew said. "They were out and about, but we lost them in the back streets, and when we realised they could be going back to the scene of the crime, we headed over there."

"They weren't there?" Tony asked.

Drew's eyes dropped. "No."

Tony paced back and forth. "The first thing we need to do is get to the hotel room, get a team to Aneeka's and Rosalee's and Carlos's to find out if they've been back. If they think we're searching for them they may think of hiding in the most obvious place on the grounds it would be the last place we'd look. Do you have surveillance on them now?"

"We did have. They went to the marina and rented a small boat. But they didn't bring it back, so we've lost them."

"Here's what we're gonna do. We're gonna hit 'em hard. We're gonna take out every place we can think of and wait. We're gonna put out an APB on all the cars we know they drive, *and* on them. Get their descriptions to every cop in the city. They have two hostages now. They either haven't gone far and have changed their car, or they've already gone. Get cops to every car rental company and flash their photos, someone will recognise them." He looked down at the paper in his hand. "For their sake, they have to."

*****

Carlos came to, tied up, gagged, and lying next to a body on a bed. The blindfold offered no ability to identify it, but he hoped it was Aneeka. He heard two men arguing in Greek and struggled to listen.

"We have to do what he says."

"But what is it he wants?"

"I don't know?"

"But he asked us to kidnap these people."

"We just do, we do not ask questions."

"But we could be in big trouble now."

"We stick it out and wait for him to call."

"What does he want with these people?"

"I don't know, but he told us to get those photos."

"We shouldn't have been so obvious. We should have done it at night then no one would have seen."

"But we didn't, and now we're trying to fix the problem."

"But the cops could find us."

"We wait for his call."

"But—"

"End of discussion!"

They fell silent, and Carlos lay back to rest. What a grade A cock-up this all was. Aneeka got kidnapped because she saw them in Rosalee's yard, and what was he kidnapped for? And where were Tony and Harry's guards? And where was he…?

*****

Teams of cops swarmed every part of town; Carlos's apartment, Aneeka's house, the hotel where, surprise,

surprise, the men had left without paying, the movie theatre, take out joints, car rental shops, and any small marina or dock up the coast.

They found the boat with blood in the bottom.

But that was all.

Nothing more; nothing less.

They kept surveillance teams in every place and moved on, hoping someone would remember something.

Had anyone seen two men carrying an unconscious porn star up the beach to the car park? Had anyone seen suspicious behaviour in the neighbourhood?

Harry put every man he had out to talk to people they knew, letting them know that Carlos had been kidnapped and if they saw anything to call him immediately. The gay community rallied, the porn community rallied, and all put ears to the ground for information while keeping the news to themselves.

Harry refused to call Carlos's parents, figuring, why disturb them with news like this when he hoped he could find Carlos and bring him home, because when push came to shove, he had grown quite fond of the boy and considered him almost as a son.

*****

The phone rang.

"Hello…yes…all right…yes…okay…yes…okay…bye."

"Was that him?"

"Yes."

"What did he want?"

"He said to wait till dark and kill the woman, burn her and her photographs, and bring the boy back to him."

"All the way to Greece?"

"No, he's not in Greece."

"Then where is he?"

"Here in United States."

An intake of breath. "He's here?"

"Yes."

And we're supposed to take him where?"

"He did not say."

"But how do we know where to take him?"

"He said to call him when job was done."

"And we have to take him in the car?"

"Of course, we cannot fly."

"But what if we are caught?"

"If we are careful we should not be."

"But surely there are people looking for us now."

"I'm sure, but we must leave under cover of dark."

"And where do we dump body?"

"There is old quarry on way. We dump her, burn her and leave."

"On way to where?"

"On way out of town."

Waiting until dark, the men loaded Aneeka and Carlos into the trunk, threw their bags in next to them, emptied their hotel room and drove out of the parking lot.

They weren't noticed.

Why would they be? It was a seedy part of town, bordering the outskirts, derelict houses, hotels, and bars. Everyone was either blind drunk or off their face on drugs.

No, they weren't noticed.

They took a circuitous route out of town, driving south out of L.A. until they found the exit that would take them back north. It was going to be a long trip, but they had to do it. Bypassing L.A. on the highway, they headed further north and took another exit back. But this one wouldn't take them completely back to L.A., it would take them out to the desert, past one horse towns and that empty quarry they needed.

They kept an eye out for cars following them and pulled over when there was too much traffic, pretending to have a break in case someone was watching. They swigged beer and cola and eventually pulled back onto the desolate highway and drove up the empty road to the quarry, coming to a stop away from the entrance where no one would see them and the fire they were about to start.

They got out, looked around, popped the trunk and hauled Aneeka's body out, carrying her a short distance to lay her down on the cold gravel and rocks.

The fresh air helped her come to, and she breathed. "Mmm," she mumbled behind her gag. "Mmm." She kicked her legs. "Mmm, mmm."

"Shut up," the short man said and gave her a swift kick in the side.

"Ahh," she screamed behind the gag. "Mmm, mmm."

"I said, shut up," he shouted.

"Knock it off, Petrov," Dimitri Yustoff said, coming over with a can of gas and matches. He'd left the trunk up and didn't see Carlos struggle out.

Carlos had spent the whole car trip untying his hands, but pretended to be out of it when they'd stopped and opened the trunk. They'd only grabbed Aneeka, so he was safe, and he'd quickly pulled off the leg rope, blindfold, and tape. He slid over the side of the trunk and hid around the back of the car out of their way. Watching them pour the fluid over Aneeka he heard her muffled cries. "Fuck!" He had to do something, and do something he did when he saw them light the match. "No," he yelled and bolted toward the two men.

Dimitri dropped the match in shock and Petrov's eyes went wide.

Carlos saw Aneeka roll away from them as he came crashing into both of them.

Petrov went down like a lead balloon, but Dimitri pushed himself away and ran for the car.

Aneeka screamed behind her gag and Carlos punched Petrov, who was beneath him, until he was dazed and then raced over to her, ripping off her gag and blindfold.

A shot rang out.

Dimitri had gotten his gun from the car and was shooting at them.

Carlos dragged Aneeka further away and she quickly sat up, pulled her legs through her arms, and started pulling the rope around her wrists with her teeth.

"Go get them," she said.

Carlos ducked and weaved his way to Dimitri and

tackled him. "Why did you do this?" he yelled. "Who told you to do this?" The gun was knocked away and they struggled. "Where were you taking us? Ugh." Dimitri had landed a punch to the chiselled jaw of Carlo Stefan. Carlos rolled off, but quickly sprang up.

Aneeka finished with her bonds as Petrov came to and she saw he was lying in the same spot she had been. Swiftly moving over to him she kicked him in the side. "Let's see how you like it," she said when he was curled into a ball. She scrambled looking for the box of matches that had been dropped and flicked one alight. Seeing the terrified look in Petrov's eyes, she tossed it into the petrol around him.

He went up like the Fourth of July, and the scream that left his throat was the guttural noise of pure hell. He rolled, and rolled, and rolled, managing to dampen the flames.

Carlos and Dimitri stopped fighting long enough to see what was happening, and that's when Carlos felt the pain in his head.

Dimitri hauled the unconscious body into the trunk, slammed the lid shut and ran to the driver's side. Firing off the rest of his bullets he saw Aneeka go down. He got in, slammed the door, gunned the engine, and sped off back to the highway to continue on to the next town to make his phone call.

Aneeka gasped. "Ah, fuck!" came out through gritted teeth. Her hand tightly grasped her right arm where the bullet had hit, and it burned like a mother. The only thing she could do was go into meditation mode.

She breathed, in and out, in and out. Slowly, surely,

her breathing regulated and the pain subsided.

Unlike the pain of the man ten feet from her.

Petrov groaned. The pain, the searing pain. He'd never been set on fire before and didn't appreciate being set on fire now. Rolling had managed to put it out, but he could feel the melting skin, the burning of his lungs. He was barely able to breathe, and it tasted like ash and smoke. Seeing her stand over him, the gorgeous black woman they had been told to take, he didn't know why they needed to get the guy with the big cock because all they'd needed to do was threaten the woman for the photos. But no, the cockhead he worked with had decided to take her and that's all there was to it. Now here he was, lying in some God forsaken hole in the ground, melting like the witch in the Wizard of Oz, and the woman they'd kidnapped was standing over him. His partner had taken off on him, and he was not going to get back home to see his wife and child. *That's what happens when you live a life of crime,* he thought. *I always thought it was a joke, that saying. Crime doesn't pay. Well, it certainly won't be paying this time.* His eyes drooped, and he was down to his last gasps of air.

Aneeka knelt down beside him, blood pouring from her arm wound, and she laid her hand on his forehead. "It's all right," she soothed. "You will be with the creator soon. You will be at peace soon."

Her calming words made him feel better as he slipped away.

Seeing his eyes close and hearing the death rattle, Aneeka stood, breathed deeply and set off for the highway. She needed a phone, she needed food, and she needed a stiff drink.

*****

Dimitri sped down the highway looking for a phone booth. He needed to make his call, needed to call his boss, needed to find out where to dump the body in the trunk. Why couldn't they have just killed them both? He banged the steering wheel with his fists. Hard calloused fists. All the years he'd worked for his boss, and nothing had ever been a cock-up like this. Sure, he'd kidnapped people before, and sure he'd killed people before, but all of this had been a cock-up from start to almost finish. And now he had to drive to God knows where to get rid of the body in the trunk. He shook his head. This thing, this plan, was getting worse and worse.

Seeing a gas station in the distance, he checked the gas gauge. He needed to fill up the old bomb of a gas guzzler, so he pulled in. Casually gazing around while pumping gas, he was on the lookout for cops, feds or suits. He saw no one and went inside to pay. He grabbed some candy bars, soda, and chips, handed over his money, peered around and walked outside. He parked beside the phone booth and made his call. "I've got him, where do I bring him?"

"Did you dispose of the woman?"

"Yes."

"And did everything go smoothly?"

"…Not quite…"

"What do you mean…not quite?"

"We lost Theodopolous."

"…And how did you do that?"

"The woman got loose and set him on fire."

"…But you still have him…"

"Yes."

"Then bring him…"

Dimitri listened and hung up. Peering around before leaving, he failed to notice the man pumping gas that just happened to be an off-duty cop who still had his APB in his car.

The man leant in and checked the photo. Yes, the same one, and after finishing with the gas went in to make a phone call to his superiors before paying and following.

*****

Aneeka hiked back to the highway and started walking. She didn't like the idea of hitchhiking but had to get a lift to the nearest phone. With no headlights in sight, she had to keep moving and pushed on against the night.

*****

Carlos woke to a pounding headache and a bumpy road. "Ugh," he groaned. "Where the hell are we?"

Thunder cracked overhead making him jump. "Great, now it's gonna rain." He felt around for something to break out of the trunk with and found some loose tools. Forcing them into the cracks and crevices of the trunk, he tried to pop it but couldn't, so he smashed out the lights instead, hoping a cop car would pull the driver over for not having brake lights. He lay back. *I hope Aneeka is okay. Can she make it on her own? It's a long walk to civilisation.* He rubbed his head. Another crack of thunder made it worse because of the electrical waves flowing through the car. *I wonder where Tony is?*

*****

Tony had been at the cop station with Drew and Star when the call came through about the sighting of Dimitri Yustoff at a gas station. They made a beeline for their cars and got on the road, even though it was nearly two hours away. The off-duty officer had said he'd continue following the car and report in periodically. They hit the gas and waited for his call.

*****

Aneeka kept walking. She'd rather walk than hitchhike with some of the crazies around these days. But her arm was killing her, and she didn't see any lights in sight. Breathing deeply she kept walking, trying to piece the puzzle together. She still couldn't figure out why they had kidnapped her. If photos were all they wanted, just ask. No need to trash her place, or take her against her will. And who was the person behind it all? They had not only taken her, but Carlos as well. Why did they want him? Did they need him for something? Did they want to frame him for Rosalee's murder again? Maybe inject him with drugs and plant a suicide note that was also a confession? Confessing that he had killed Rosalee when he hadn't?

Her head pounded to a different beat than her arm, so she breathed slowly and deeply. *What I wouldn't give for a drink and maybe some aspirin,* she thought. She kept on walking, one foot in front of the other. How far now? How long had she been walking? She tried to picture the highway, but didn't know which highway she was on. After pounding up a hill she stopped. There, in the distance, the bright lights of a city. "Ah," she said. "Vegas!"

The thunder cracked overhead.

*****

Dimitri pushed through. The most direct way to get past Vegas was through Vegas, so he hit the strip and kept going. *God, I wish I could stop just for one game, one drink, one woman,* he thought, eyeing off the women walking the streets. He hadn't had a fuck in weeks and had been tempted to do damage to the black woman, but he had refrained, although, he had allowed himself to touch her. She was unconscious, just how he liked them, and he'd had a suck of her tits, but nothing else.

And then when they got the porn king he couldn't help himself. He had to have a look at the great cock in person. It was long and strong and sturdy, and he'd held it, feeling the weight in his hand.

Mmm, he'd thought. *Not much heavier than mine.* Now he had the king of cock in his trunk. He drove out the other side of Vegas and kept going. It was going to be a long drive and would take a couple of days, but he had to get there, and since Theodopolous wasn't there to help with the driving, he was going to have to do it all himself. Which meant no sleep. Just sugar, fresh air, and coffee.

*****

Aneeka came across the gas station, saw it in the distance, and broke into a stumbling run. There was no way she was giving up now with help in sight, and she ran as hard as she could.

The station came closer.

She ran faster.

The gas station attendant walked outside to check on something and saw a black woman running at him.

"Help me, please help me," Aneeka yelled. "I've been shot." She ran into the station and fell just as a car came screeching in.

*****

Harry stormed around his office while Harriet, Connie, and Viv sat on the sofa. "How long does it take to find someone, God in blazes?" The phone rang. Harry grabbed it in a second. "Yes."

"He's heading to Vegas at this stage," Tony said. "No word on Aneeka or Carlos, but one of the men has been identified."

"Okay, keep me informed." Harry replaced the phone

and resumed his pacing. "He's been taken to Vegas."

Harriet fluttered her handkerchief. "What is going on Harry? Why would someone do this?"

"I don't know, but I won't rest until I find out."

*****

Tony had to stop for gas, but Star and Drew hadn't, so they left him and kept going. He took a minute to call Harry then jumped in his car and raced off, knowing he'd easily catch up.

*****

"What the hell!" Drew flew out of the car and ran to Aneeka's side. "Ms Ne Masta, are you all right?"

Star bailed up the attendant. "What did you do? What did you do?"

"It wasn't him," Aneeka said. "It was the men and one's dead. They tried to kill me, set me on fire. But Carlos tackled them, and it ended up being one of them that was on fire. The other took off with Carlos. He shot at me." She looked at her arm. "He got me."

Five cars pulled in behind them.

"Where did all of this happen?" Drew put his coat around her.

"In a quarry," she said. "Back that way. He's still there."

"Get cars back to the quarry and look for him, boys. It's one of the men we're after," Star barked, hands on hips and thinking he was in charge.

Drew helped Aneeka to her feet as Tony slammed

into the station.

"Aneeka!"

"Tony." She ran for him and he enveloped her in a bear hug.

"Are you okay?" he asked. "Harry's mad as hell about this."

"No, I'm not," she said and showed him her arm. "I've been shot."

Tony examined it. "Just a flesh wound, let's get it wrapped up." He led her inside and Star and Drew followed.

"Start from the beginning and leave nothing out," Star demanded as Drew questioned the attendant.

"I was taken from my own backyard," Aneeka said as Tony bathed her wound with products he'd grabbed from the store's shelves. "My eyes and mouth were covered, my arms and legs bound. They held me somewhere and demanded the photos I'd taken. I wondered what their interest in the photos was, and realised they must be the men in them. They knocked me out, and I only came to when they put me on the ground in the quarry. I fought, Carlos got my blindfold off, and I untied myself while he was fighting one of the men. The other one ended up on fire because he was lying in the petrol they had poured on me. He must have rolled onto the matches because he went up in a ball of flame," she lied as the rain came pouring down hard outside.

They all looked out the window for a few moments.

"Do you have any idea why they want a porn actor?" Star asked.

She looked up at him as Tony finished wrapping her arm. "No."

"Any idea where they're going?"

"No."

"All right, Vega," Star said to Tony. "Get her back home safely and we'll see after the actor."

"You've clearly forgotten Star that *your* superior put *me* in charge. *Not you,*" Tony reminded him.

Star flinched and went beet red.

"You do as *I* say," Tony continued. "*We* will go after Carlos. Aneeka, do you want to go back?" He looked at her for her answer.

"No." She shook her head. "I want to continue. I want to know what's going on."

"Then you'll come with me," Tony said, helping her stand. "Have we heard from the off-duty cop yet?" he asked Star who just stared at him with a look that could freeze Satan in hell and then shatter him into a million pieces. It didn't faze Tony, who'd faced worse.

"Word is he just called in. They pulled into a fast food outlet and are continuing on their way," Star finally said.

"To where?"

Drew came over. "He's in Utah at the moment. Who knows where he's going."

"Okay, let's take the same road he's taking and keep up," Tony said. "Stock up on food, water and whatever you need. Let's get on the road. I'm going to call Harry, sit tight," he told Aneeka and went to make the call.

When his back was turned Star bolted for the car

and jumped behind the wheel.

Drew followed and jumped in after him. "What are you doing? We have to wait."

"The hell we are," snarled Star and they skidded out of the station. "Who does that pompous, no good, low-down son of a cock sucking bitch think he is?" Star spat.

"The person in charge," Drew replied. "Shouldn't we wait?"

"Fuck waiting. I'm a cop," Star ranted, stepping on the gas. "I'll do whatever the fuck I want and to fucking hell with that cock sucker."

"Until Ward gets on your case and demotes you."

Star seethed, the rain poured down, and Drew hung on.

Tony got through to Harry. "I've got Aneeka, she's okay. She was nicked by a bullet, but she'll be fine."

"Oh, thank God." Harry slumped in his chair. "What about the boy?"

"Still got him."

"Get Aneeka back here."

"No, she wants to continue so I'm taking her."

"Take care of her then."

"I will."

"Keep me updated."

Tony hung up and made his way back to Aneeka. After leading her to the car, he made her comfortable and was pissed that the detectives had taken off, but not surprised that Star was acting out. He sped onto the highway in the same direction with two cop cars after him.

"Pair of fucking idiots." He slammed the wheel. "His boss threatened to demote him and he still acts like a cock."

"What did Harry say?" Aneeka changed the subject.

"Thank God you're okay and to take care of you and find the boy."

"He's hardly a boy."

"To me he is," he spat. "A selfish, inconsiderate little asshole who doesn't think twice about anybody but himself."

"So, like you when you were that age." Aneeka flashed a grin.

Tony's jaw tightened. "I *was not* like that when I was his age, and what would you know about it, anyway?"

"I've heard stories."

"Not from me you haven't, and not from anybody else."

"And why do you think that?"

He glanced at her. "Because *nobody* knows about my past."

*****

Back at Harry's, everyone heaved a sigh of relief except for Vivian who felt sick to her stomach. She stood up. "Uh, excuse me. I feel sick. It must be all the stress." She fled to a bathroom and promptly threw up in the toilet. When she was done, she flushed and rinsed off. Patting her face with cold water at the sink, she thought about the mess that was happening right now and said a quick prayer that Carlos was found alive and well and came home safely.

She dried her face and opened her purse for her compact, seeing the stick at the bottom of the bag where she'd thrown it that morning.

The stick from the pregnancy kit.

*****

Rain bucketed down through Vegas into Utah, and the pounding on the trunk was not helping the pounding in Carlos's head. He was cramped. His legs bent at odd angles, and something was digging into his back. He shifted, trying to find a more comfortable position, but his five-ten frame didn't fit well in the trunk of a car.

I wonder how long we've been driving for… His eyes closed as the rain came to a stop.

The off-duty officer pulled in at the rest stop, staying out of view of the other car. There were tables, a phone, a picnic bench and barbecue, and he went into the toilet block for a quick check. Seeing no one else, he called in to his boss. "We're at a truck stop in Colorado. I'm still following and have no idea where he's going. I'll need to stop for gas at the next station, so I'll let you know where."

Dimitri slept with one ear open and a gun in his hand. *Thank God for quiet nights and good hearing,* he thought and wound up his window.

*****

When the sun's rays hit the horizon, Dimitri woke, and after taking a quick leak, he took off for the main road. He knew where he was going, but the man behind him didn't. He had plenty of places to lead him, but not much time to do it in. He had another day, maybe two, to get to his destination, so if he stopped for gas and food and nothing else, he should make good time.

Driving into the first gas station he came across, he got out to pump his own gas, keeping an eye out for the car which he saw pull in front of the toilet block. He casually leant on his car giving a periodical glance over his shoulder. After racking up a thirty dollar bill, he added to it with coffee and bagels and took a few minutes to watch the tall, lanky man get his own food and, gas up.

He threw his rubbish in the bin and took off for his destination.

The off-duty cop called in. "I'm at a small gas station in Nebraska. It's a little town, not much, gotta go." He jumped in his car and followed.

*****

Two hours behind were Star and Drew, Tony and Aneeka, and five cop cars. Occasionally there'd be reports on the car from officers seeing it drive by. They radioed in and back to L.A. Ward had set up a map to keep track of his movements with red tacks. "He's heading cross country," he radioed the detectives. "Probably Iowa and Illinois next. I'll get in contact with Chicago PD in case he comes their way, and they can keep an eye out."

"What if he's heading for New York?" Star asked on the two-way. "Or takes a right or left and heads in a different direction?"

"Then we'll be ready," Ward said. "Sit on his tail and close in. Out."

Star hung up the handset. "How long are we meant to follow?"

"As long as we have to," Drew said. "Not that it matters."

*****

Aneeka woke from her restless sleep and looked around. Stretching, she winced, having forgotten about her arm.

"You okay?" Tony asked. "There's some water and aspirin if you need it."

She smiled. "What would I do without you?" She cracked open the aspirin, swallowed three and washed them down with water.

"A damn sight better than what's happened with Carlos Stephanopoulos," he said. "There's been nothing but trouble since that boy came to town."

"And yet, somehow I don't think it's his fault." She sipped more water.

"Huh?" Tony grunted. *"How is it not his fault?"*

"Because I think someone is doing it *to* him like they did it to me."

He glanced at her. "What makes you say that?"

"Why did they take me? Because I caught them on camera and told the police. Why did they try to set

Carlos up? Because someone wanted him in trouble. So who is doing this? Who is behind it?"

Tony sighed. "Dunno. Maybe Harry's investigators have found something out."

*****

One by one, they trailed across the countryside into Iowa to reach the border of Illinois where Dimitri stopped for gas. He was close now, not far to go, but he needed gas and food and a leak and a fuck. He parked around the back of the station after filling the tank and quickly ate the burger he'd bought, slurped down his drink, and kept an eye out for a female who might be up for it. He saw no one but the guy in the car. The one that had been following him since Vegas. He watched the man go into the station and took the opportunity to pop the trunk to check on the porn star. He nudged him.

"Ugh," Carlos groaned, his hand moving slowly up to his head. "What's…what's happening?"

"I'm done with you, Mr Ten Inch Cock. I am *so* done with you," he hissed and slammed the lid shut. "Don't worry, not long now and then *he* can take you."

*****

"You'd better step on it, he's made Illinois." Ward's voice popped up over the radio. "I've called the Captain, they know not to stop him at any time and to let him go. We need to find out where he's going."

"Why are we not nabbing him if he has a body in

the trunk?" Star asked.

"Because there's a reason this is happening, so there must be bigger fish to fry. Besides, I take orders too, you know."

Star hung up. "Why in fuck's name is this happening?"

"Don't know, but it's your turn to drive." Drew pulled over into a station and the others followed. They wasted no more than five minutes getting gas, food or taking a leak, then it was back on the road at more speed.

*****

Harry got off the phone with his investigators.

"Well?" Harriet asked, running her pearls through her hand.

"They're on the trail. They've checked back in Mykonos, nothing there. They've checked back in all the places the cops have been, nothing, but…" He waved a finger. "They have found out something very interesting. There is a private plane registered to a Greek company out of Athens that flew into O'Hare Airport three days ago."

"Is that important?" Connie asked. She had camped out at Harry's since this started.

"Well…" Harry paced. "It may or may not be. But, since it's from Athens, and Carlos is from Mykonos, I wonder. Of course, the CEOs could just be here on business, but there's a name that's popped up that we know from Carlos's last lot of trouble."

"And who's that?" Viv asked, clutching her

handkerchief to her mouth.

"Gustoff Dropopolous."

"And who's he?" Harriett asked.

"The man at the resort that claimed Carlos raped two women and then shot one."

Connie's eyes widened. "Oh, my God. That means I could have seen him."

"Did you?" Harry asked.

She shook her head slowly. "I don't think so."

"Did *he* see *you*?"

Another shake. "I don't think so, otherwise he might have attacked us at the pier and he didn't."

Harry stood in front of her. "Well, the fact that he's still around is highly suspicious, and my men are on it. I'll let Tony know the next time he calls in."

"What will he be able to do?"

"Pass it on to the cops," Harry said.

*****

Dimitri headed into a massive storm as he crossed Illinois and hoped it didn't slow him down. He had to stop to make a call and take a leak. "All that damn coffee and soda," he muttered and stopped outside of the next gas station he came across. He took a leak and entered the phone booth, keeping an eye out for the car. "I'm nearly there, where do I go?"

"The airport."

"Which one?"

"O'Hare."

"And then what?"

"We deal with it."

"What time?" He looked at his watch.

"Eight-thirty, sharp."

He sighed. "I'll do my best."

*****

Tony believed they'd made good time and phoned Harry during a break. Learning of the name Gustoff Dropopolous, he asked Star and Drew if they'd heard of it.

"Don't remember that one," Drew said, pumping the gas.

"And it wasn't the name of either man involved in the kidnapping," Star added. "So who is he?"

"Someone of interest," Tony said. "Let's get going."

*****

Dimitri cruised toward the city of Chicago. Rain bucketed down so he had to slow down, but he knew that gave the others a chance to gain on him. "Damn it." He banged the steering wheel and looked at his watch. Seven forty-five. He had forty-five minutes to get to the airport. Glancing in the rear-view mirror, he saw the car behind him had moved closer, but also noticed something strange. There was a car cruising on each side of the car going at the exact same pace. Never ahead, never behind. Three cars abreast on the highway. He didn't like the look of that. Glancing back at his watch he pressed the accelerator.

Carlos came to as the rain belted down on the trunk. The noise deafened him, making him grab his pounding brain. "Ugh, God." He groaned. "Where are we? Why am I still in the trunk?" Breathing deeply, he decided enough was enough.

"Fuck it! I gotta get 'em off my tail." Dimitri sped up, heading into the heart of the city. "I gotta lose 'em and lose 'em now." He'd skirted the airport because if he'd gone straight there, they would have followed and found not only him but his boss. And he couldn't risk it. Veering left then right, dodging traffic and pedestrians, he sped through the city.

*****

"We're heading for Chicago, now," Star told Ward. "Are the cops on his tail?"

"They're keeping an eye on him and following, trying to clean up the mess."

"Well, we're nearly there, any idea where he's going?"

"Not yet, but hurry up."

Tony heard the conversation on his two-way. He was only a hundred yards or so behind the detectives and sped up. That was the thrill of the chase; he was going and closing in.

"Whoa." Aneeka grabbed the dashboard. "Guess there's no point asking you to slow down?"

"Nope. Just hang on."

*****

Carlos was being tossed around in the trunk, but managed to find a metal bar that he could get his fingers around. He braced himself with one foot and started kicking at the back seat with the other. They swerved left then right, and he kicked again, and again, and again. The seat gave way, but not all the way. He rested as they swerved around a corner.

*****

"He's headed north out of the city," blasted over the two-way.

"Nearly have him now," Star and Tony said at the same time. "You're going down cock sucker!"

*****

Dimitri was trying not to panic. It was eight oh five and he had twenty-five minutes to get the cock sucker in his trunk to the airport, but needed to get the cops off his tail. He looked in the rear-view. There were flashing lights behind the three cars. "Fuck it! Fuck it, fuck it, fuck it." He slammed the wheel and did a screeching turn down the next main road he came to, having no idea where he was, but saw planes landing and taking off in the distance. He changed lanes and thunder clapped overhead, covering the sound of Carlos finally kicking through the back seat.

Carlos rested, listening to the man mutter and heard the word cops. *God, are they behind us? Is that why he's driving like a mad man?* He quietly pushed the seat aside and carefully crawled through, inch by inch. First his arms, then his head and chest. He pulled his legs up as they swerved around a corner and waited until the car had settled before pulling them out. He lay on the back seat listening.

"Gotta get to the airport. Where the fuck is O'Hare?" He wildly swung the wheel and Carlos grabbed the armrest. "Gotta get to the airport. Gotta get to the airport. Where the fuck is the turn for the airport? What the fuck? What the fuck is...no, no, no." He banged the wheel. He'd seen the cars with sirens and flashing lights bearing down on him, in front of him as he glanced in the rear-view, bearing down from behind him. Sweat dripped down his face, his back, his sides. "No, no, no," he yelled.

Carlos took his chance and popped his head up to look. Seeing the cop cars, he took his chance at exactly the same time the man saw him in the rear-view.

"No," he yelled as Carlos leant over the seat and grabbed the steering wheel. "No." The wheel lurched back and forth, sending the car careening across the road and back. "No, get off me," Dimitri yelled, letting one hand off the wheel to punch Carlos in the face. "Get back, let go of the wheel."

Carlos hung on. "No! Tell me who you are and who you're working for. Who told you to do this?"

O'Hare came up in the distance.

So did the cop cars.

"Fuck you and your ten inch cock, you cock sucking asshole," Dimitri yelled as they both wrenched the wheel and smashed through the bridge railing into the cold Illinois water.

*****

Star and Drew could only stare in shock and amazement as the car flew off the bridge no more than a hundred feet in front of them, and Star could swear he saw two faces in the front seat. They screeched to a stop at the gaping hole in the railing.

"No," Aneeka screamed.

They had all been tearing down the road, closing in on the car, lights flashing, sirens blaring, in the pouring rain when they saw the car go off the bridge.

"Fucking hell," Tony yelled. "Hang on." He screeched to a halt behind the detectives, and they all raced out of their cars to stare over the railing.

*****

The last thing Carlos saw was the bright lights of the cars in his face, blinding him. He and Dimitri hung on to the wheel as the car crashed through the barrier and into the cold water below. Letting go of the wheel, he pushed backwards, away from the windshield as it crashed in.

Water engulfed the car, flowing over Dimitri and Carlos as he pushed back to the back window. He needed as much air as possible, but the car was filling up fast.

Dimitri struggled and found his jacket caught on the door, but yanking it, he couldn't get it free. His lungs burned, his head pounded, and tugging on his jacket wasn't getting him out of there.

Carlos took a deep breath before water flowed over his head. Once the car was under, he moved to Dimitri and yanked his arm. The car lights flickered, but Dimitri saw Carlos point upward. Dimitri tugged his jacket, but couldn't break free.

Carlos started yanking it off him, and Dimitri realised what he meant and slid his arms out of the jacket.

The car settled on the bottom of the river and Carlos pushed Dimitri through the windscreen and followed him out, pushing and pulling him to the surface.

Dimitri pushed him away, kicking off and swimming for the surface.

Carlos didn't bother following him; he needed air now. Living on Mykonos for the last ten years had afforded him good swimming skills and the ability to hold his breath for four minutes, but this was hitting his limits. He no longer saw the man, but saw the lights as he surfaced. "Argh." He gulped in air.

"Carlos," Tony and Aneeka yelled out. "Carlos."

Sucking in huge gulps of air he looked up and saw everyone holding their flashlights down on him. They waved towards their right, his left, and he saw the bank only metres from him. He swam for it in the pouring rain and freezing water, using every water skill he had and what little energy he had left to get him there.

Tony and Aneeka ran for it with Star and Drew and all the cops after them. They ran across the bridge, over the side, and down the bank to haul a shivering

Carlos out of the water. Tony whipped off his jacket and put it around his shoulders. "Carlos. Carlos, are you all right? Are you hurt?"

"No." Carlos coughed up some river water. "I'm okay." They helped him to the bridge. "Where is he? The driver." He frantically looked around. "Where is he?" he yelled.

"Get your flashlights down to the bank and start searching," Star yelled. "Get over the other side and look for a body."

Tony checked Carlos over for cuts and damage.

"I'm okay." Carlos pushed his hand away. "I'm just…"

"Yes?" Aneeka took his face in her hands.

"Tired and hungry." He smiled softly.

"Let's get you to the car. We're gonna get you home." Tony and Aneeka led him back to their car.

"There's no body." Star raced up to them. "No body, nothing. He either floated off down the river, or got out on the other bank. So if he did, where the fuck is he heading?"

A plane flew overhead.

"The airport."

Everyone looked at Carlos.

"What did you say?" Tony asked.

Carlos looked at him. "The airport. O'Hare. He had to get to O'Hare."

"Let's get to O'Hare," Star yelled. "Everyone to the airport."

Tony bundled Carlos into the back seat, and Aneeka piled in after him. She clung to him as they belted down the highway and onto the road that led to the airport.

"Did he say anything to you?" she asked. "Who he was? Why they wanted you? *What* they wanted?"

Carlos shook his head and rubbed it when pain surged through it. "No. Once we had left that place where they were going to kill you, I was in the trunk and in and out of it. God, I need something for this headache." Tony threw aspirin and a bottle of water into the back seat and he grabbed them and downed three.

*****

"I'm coming," Dimitri yelled, running through the back of the airport to the hanger that held the private plane that would take him back to Greece. "I'm coming." He saw it on the tarmac, stairs down, waiting in the pouring rain. "Wait for me, I'm coming." He'd made it to the other side of the river bank and managed to grab a taxi to the airport, finding a back way in when he'd shoved a gun in the driver's face. Time was running out, and he needed to get on that plane. His breath was leaving him. After dealing with the fight, the crash, and shivering, which he was not used to, he didn't have much left. He saw a man stick his head out of the door. "I'm coming," he yelled, waving his arm.

The man popped his head back in, and a few seconds later his boss popped out and looked in his direction. A look as black as the night they were in crossed his face and he receded into the plane. The rotors revved, the first man popped back out, and a look of surprise flitted across his face.

Dimitri looked behind him and saw the flashing lights. "No," he yelled and ran faster.

The man on the plane held out his arm, and a small flash went off.

Dimitri Yustoff fell dead on the tarmac.

"Oh, my God, did you just see that?" Carlos said, leaning forward in his seat. "They just shot him."

The stairs closed, the rotors buzzed, and the plane took off for the runway.

"Stop it," Star yelled. "Get in front of it," he told Drew. "Get in front of it."

"I've got my foot on the floor," Drew yelled back, speeding down the back road and past the dead man.

The plane took off for the runway, and he screeched to a halt.

"What the fuck are you stopping for?" Star screamed. "After them, after them."

"It's too dangerous," Drew yelled. "We'd never make it, and there are too many other planes here. It's too dangerous."

Tony slammed on the brakes behind them, and they piled out.

Carlos ran back to the man and rolled him. "That's him. That's the man in the car."

Thunder cracked overhead, and they watched the plane take off.

Carlos, Tony, and Aneeka walked over to the detectives as Star was still screeching. The rain poured down, soaking them to the skin, plastering their clothes to their bodies as the plane flew off into the middle of the thunderous sky.

"What now?" Carlos asked.

"Mother fucker," Star screamed, kicking at his car's tyre. "Mother fucking son of a cock sucking bitch."

"What now?" Carlos repeated more firmly.

Drew glanced at him. *"Find out who was on that plane, why they were here, what they wanted with you and where they're going."*

Carlos sighed. "Is that all?" He pushed his hair back with both hands. "What a fucking cock-up."

They lost sight of the plane as Star finally exerted all of his energy by giving the tyre one final kick and bending over, hands on knees. "Mother fuckers," he gasped, hating the stitch that was now in his side. He stood, not straight, as his back was also killing him. Huffing and puffing, he walked around the group and stood by Carlos, looking past him back toward the hangers. He saw a group of cops, feds and other people with two young guys at the head of the pack standing on the tarmac looking at them. "Hey," he said to Carlos and pointed toward the group. "Friends of yours?"

Carlos turned and recognised the two young men in front instantly.

About the Author

L.J. has been writing since 2006, when her first of many novels, ***The Road To Vegas,*** was born. In 2016 she created the ***Porn Star Brothers*** series about three sizzlingly hot Australian born Greek Island raised brothers who became the hottest porn stars in '70s America.

L.J. lives in Australia, loves '80s music, disaster movies, and collecting Jackie Collins books as Jackie is her inspiration and mentor.

L.J. Diva is the adult pen name for author Tiara King. You can find more about Tiara on her website; follow her on social media, or visit her publishing house, Royal Star Publishing.

Socials

tiaraking.com.au/ljdiva

royalstarpublishing.com.au

Sign up for *Tiara's* Newsletter…

Make sure you're always in the know and never miss free exclusives, the latest news, book updates, and so much more with newsletters from…

tiaraking.com.au

Have you read these?

The Porn Star Brothers Series

Carlos: Book 1
Pedro: Book 2
Tomas: Book 3
Retribution: Book 4
Porn Star Brothers
Forever
Love Never Dies
Stefan: The New Generation
DeLuca
Spiros & Jenny
And Always

The Illicit Things Series

Her
Him
Madam X

A Novel Investigation Series

Designs in Crime
A Killer Plot
Murder on the Set
A Novel Investigation (omnibus)

Or these?

NOVELS

Burning Desires
Anything for You
Falling for London
The Road to Vegas
Hollywood Dreams
The Billionaire's Dirty Little Secret

SHORT STORIES

The Body
The Perfect Plot
The Star of Your Own Crime Scene